Thomas Siddell

Gunnerkrigg Court™

Research

Published by
ARCHAIA™

Written & Illustrated by

Thomas Siddell

Designer
Scott Newman

Editor
Dafna Pleban

BOOM! Studios, 5670 Wilshire Boulevard, Suite 450, Los Angeles, CA 90036-5679. Printed in China. First Printing.

Softcover Edition
ISBN: 978-1-60886-762-2
eISBN: 978-1-61398-433-8
First Edition, First Printing.

Hardcover Edition
ISBN: 978-1-60886-763-9
eISBN: 978-1-61398-434-5
Second Edition, First Printing.

Table of Contents

Gunnerkrigg Court

Chapter 15:

Red Returns

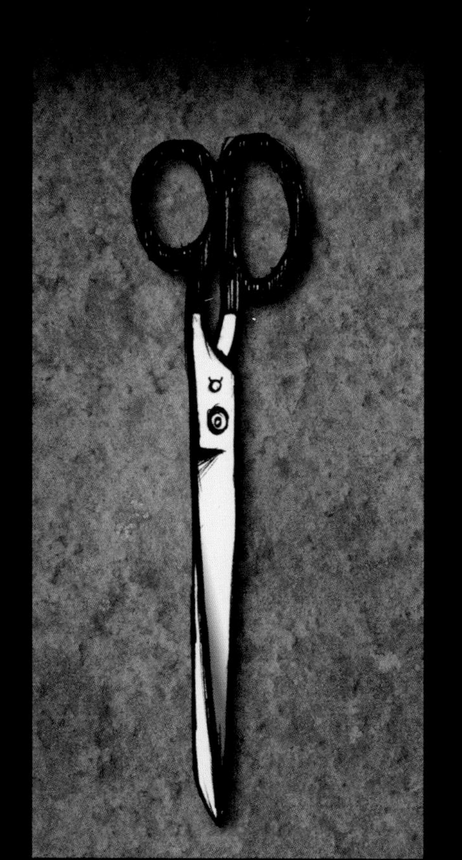

throughout the summer I realised the similarities between **Gunnerkrigg Court** and **Good Hope**, the hospital in which I used to live.
she'll be here soon!
I can't wait!
me neither!
PLAP PLAP PLAP
sometimes, in the winding, never ending corridors...
I could imagine I was at home.
PLAP PLAP PLAP

a while into the holiday I was moved to the new dorms.
they were situated much farther into the court
and I moved in before anyone else
but even then it did not take me long to feel settled.
CARVER

there was, however, one thing I never had in good hope.
KNOCK KNOCK
BONJOORNAY!
ah! annie, what's wrong?!

n~nothing, why?

a true friend.

Oh, Kat, It's wonderful!
What is it, Annie?!
It's a masquerade ball mask.
People sometimes wear them at parties, Shadow 2.
There were so many nice ones! I got one too.
I bet yours has feathers.
And a li'l beak!
Haha!

here is something for you.
ooh, what's inside?
Whaa?! so many tiny paper stars!
XL
how long did this take you?!
well... about six weeks.
haha...
uh...
and he didn't even call or anything, the whole time?
no.
annie...
I know.
well, I'm not leaving you here on your own again.

at least I wasn't completely alone.
oh yeah. shadow 2 is sounding much better now!
annie and I have been practicing a lot!
he and robot are best friends now.
and reynardine? he's being pretty quiet.
oh, he's in the **naughty zone** right now.
he's not allowed to speak.
isn't that right, reynardine?
you just bought yourself another hour, mister!

the day before year 8 began, the rest of the students arrived.
there was an assembly to welcome us to the start of a new year.
man, talk about BOOORING!
that residential sounds interesting.
yeah! a whole week of camping!
It's you!

I almos' dint recognise you wid all dat **crap** on your face!
hey!
you tricked me!
you said dis place was fun, but **it ain't!**
oh! you're that fairy from the river!
I used to be soooo beautiful!
now lookit me!

lookit how faaat I am!!

stop that! why are you doing that?!
argh!!

and look at my big, stupid face!
and my hair!
my hair!
It don't stick up no more!
annie, this girl is insane!

I'm all alone! all alone because of my hair!
you're alone because **you're insane!**

Isn't your friend with you?
the, um... blue one?

ahh! don't talk about her!

there she is!

she won't be my friend anymore!

ah!
hello again!

shaddap, you!

oh, just go away!

no, you go away!
come back!

RRaaRRghh! I hate her **so much!**
I wish she was my friend!

damn my hair to hell and back and some other places too!
KICK!

I'm sure your hair isn't the only reason she's avoiding you.
perhaps if you calmed down a little...
no! It's my hair!
she always loved my hair and now that it ain't all sticky uppy she hates me!
I want to die! for propers this time!
well, you can always get your hair cut.
But I don't think that...
what? I can get my hair what?!
cut.
If it is shorter you can make it stick up... I suppose.
you can do that? you can cut hair?!
yeah, I was gonna get mine done today.
you can come with us if you like.

UNDERGROUND

WAY OUT

these trains are so nice and quiet.

pff, that's because it's a **maglev**. all the trains in the court are.

so, how have you... been?
I'll tell ya how I bin!
I bin junk!
ever since I got here we gotta sit in these big boxes...
you mean rooms?
on these weird sitty~downy things...
uh... chairs?
and listen to some crumbum who thinks dey know everything but really they don't know diddly!
teachers
hang on a sec, how can you understand magnetic levitation but not know what a chair is?
hey alls I know is what dey tells me.

EXIT
are there lots of students who used to be fairies?
nah. just us girls in foley house.
what about the boys?
oh they were a bunch of different stuff.
one guy was a fish! haha!
whrr
whrrr
and how come you guys are wearing uniforms already?
school doesn't start properly 'til tomorrow.
whrr
huh? we always wear dem. school hain't never finished.
whrr
whrr
you mean you didn't get a summer holiday?!
a what~er what~iday?!

so when did you um... pass your test?

oh, a few minutes right after when you left.
good ol' **ysengrin** helped us pass.

ysengrin was down there?
ayup! he came to look at that metal bird dealie.

annie, I thought you said ysengrin didn't find that bird until **months** after I picked you up.

that's right. are you sure he saw it?

sure's am sure!
he went right to it an' buried dat sucka!

then I guess he was hungry
thank you that is all I need to know!

Clip Clop
noise! war seemed a civil game
proar; horrid confusion heaped
fusion rose. and now all heaven
so this means ysengrin was lying.
he doesn't sound very trustworthy.
do you know much about him?
and in whose hand
second omnipotence
two days as we com
nah. us guys who take da test live separate from da rest of da forest.
so we can learn how to be human
suffered
ding this great war,
end it. into thee such virtue and
and how to talk all proper nice like sorted.
TRUNDLE

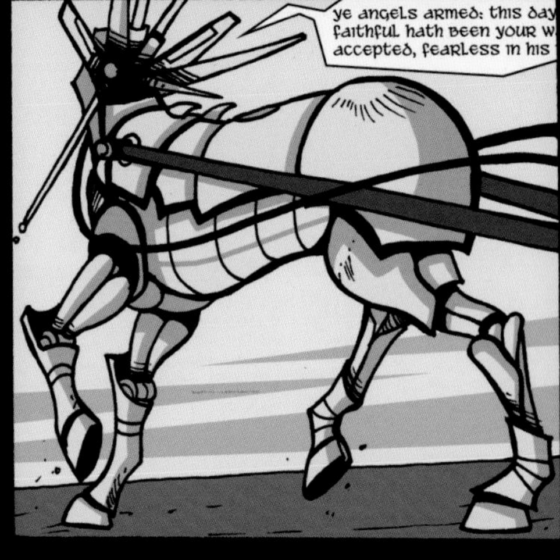
ye angels armed: this day
faithful hath been your
accepted, fearless in his

here we are!

thank you my dear.
okay so what now?
I'll go first. It's easy.
here will I wait and wish your dreams are fulfilled

very soon
ta~daa!

very nice, kat.
aah! didn't that hurt?!

huh? of course not!

dis is amazing! I had no idea you could cut stuff off these bodies!

I gotta try dis!

no!

yeah! now me! do the thing! to the hair!
how would you like it?
what? make my hair stick up!
up!
but how long do you want it?
why should I care about that!
make it stick up!
what is this?!
very well.
soon, after what I'm sure would have been a very amusing haircut montage

EEEK!
I LOOK fantastic again!

stupendous I tells ya!

Lets blow this popsicle stand, I got a friend to make!

WHAM

you know...

one of us is going to have to explain to her that she'll need like a whole can of mousse every day to keep her hair like that.

ahem

ah, hello, hello! It was nice to see you again earlier.

thank you, you as well.
listen, I'm here about your friend...

oh, her.
she's not my friend.
I don't want anything to do with her anymore.
she's changed since we passed the test.

she just wants to talk.
please give her a chance.

I can tell she misses you terribly.

Look, you can't expect her to be your friend again just cos you changed your hair.
yes I can!
now that it sticks up again she's gonna want to be my friend again straight away
Bam!
no! you have to be nice to her!
annie and I are friends because we respect each other and enjoy each other's company.
yeah well that's because yer a bunch of weird faces.
all that's too complicated.
you mark my words, mister, wassername is gonna see me and come crawlin' right back!
you don't even know her name?!

Click
Gasp!
your hair!
my hair!

It goes up again!
It goes up again!

Oooh! I want to be your friend!
Oh please!

ahahaha!

please oh please let me be your friend!
hahaha!

you better do everything I say!
yes, of course!

Like, all my homework and everything!
yes, yes!

hahahaha!
so long, JERKS!

SLAM

wow...
What a

Gunnerkrigg Court

The Wonderful Plan

perchance she is not coming back?
hmm.

maybe she has reconciled with her old friend?

if so then this makes me happy.
yes. I, also, am happy.

too happy to wang tomatoes at them?
well now, I did not say that...

Gunnerkrigg Court

Chapter 16:

A Ghost Story

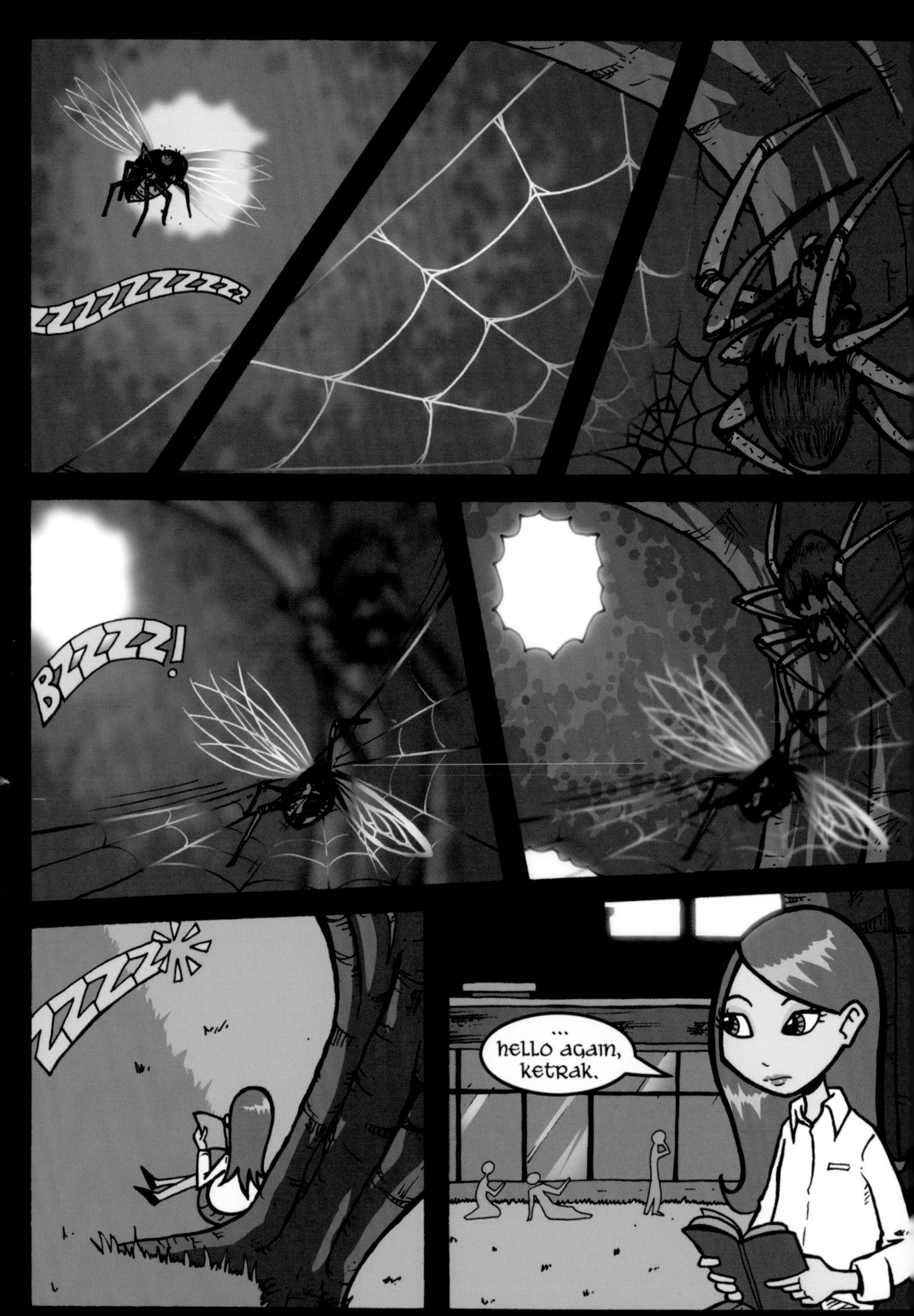
ZZZZZZZZZZZZZ
BZZZZ!
ZZZZZ
...
hello again,
ketrak.

there was no need to stop and see me.
I'm sure you are immensely busy as always.
hey, who're you talkin' to?

kat, do you remember I told you about **psychopomps**?
uh, those guys who escort dead dudes to the afterlife?

yes.
ketrak, the insect guide has paid me a visit.

you see, a fly was just killed by a spider in this tree.

say, uh...
I don't see him.
do you want to?
yeah, sure, why no~
aIEEEE!
aaahh!
ahaha hahaha!
h~how rude of me! n~nice to meet you, sir!
yes, I also think it might be best if you left. goodbye, ketrak.
he's gone now.
uuhhh! I need new eyes and a new brain!

you seemed like you wanted to get rid of him pretty quick.
yes, well.
you don't talk about those guys much.
what's it like? talking to them.
they stop by now and then. usually it's ketrak.
since something has to **die** nearby.
yeesh.
I suppose I'm used to their presence.
ever since meeting **muut** that first time in good hope.

hello!
I like your face!
why, thank you. ah! but you are surma's daughter.
you know my m... mother?
I do. she is a very gifted individual.
I am going to visit a friend in room 426. would you like to come?
mrs.tolikna? you are just in time! my da... father said she is leaving tomorrow.
457
she's kind of old though. she's probably asleep right now.
not this night.

and you didn't know what you were visiting those people for?
no, not at first. I just assumed we were visiting friends.
and this muut guy...
he ah... has an owl head and doesn't wear a shirt, you say?
steady on there, girl!
haha!
so that's all you guys did? just visit people?
not always.
one night, shortly after meeting muut...

she is so young.
I already allow you to take her on your visits.
does she really need this?
you know I would be of no use to you. not anymore.
come now, you knew it was inevitable.
sooner rather than later, yes, dear?
all she got to do is be there. the rest will sort itself out.
if you was to come the matter would be settled right quick.
antimony. come up here, poppet.

oooh, a doggie.
dearest, this is **mallt-y-nos** and the **moddey dhoo.**
evenin'
they are having a problem, you see. a dispute.

would you like to help them?
yes.

then you must always remember one thing...

SO GOOD OF YEH TO COME, PUP. TIME WEARS THIN.

CHILD, THERE IS A BOY HERE IN THE HOSPITAL WHO HAS LOST HIS WAY.

HE SHOULD BE COMING WITH ME BUT THIS **MANGEY MUTT** HERE IS ALSO TRYING TO CLAIM HIM.

QUIT YER NOISE, YEH OLD BAT! THE BOY HAS EVERY RIGHT TO CHOOSE TWIXT YOU'ER I.

THERE WERE A MOST DISFORTUNATE ACCIDENT. HIS FAMILY WAS TAKEN RIGHT AWAY BUT THE BOY WAS BROUGHT HERE TO GOOD 'OPE.

IS HE SICK?
NOT ANYMORE. BUT NOW HE'S **STUCK.**

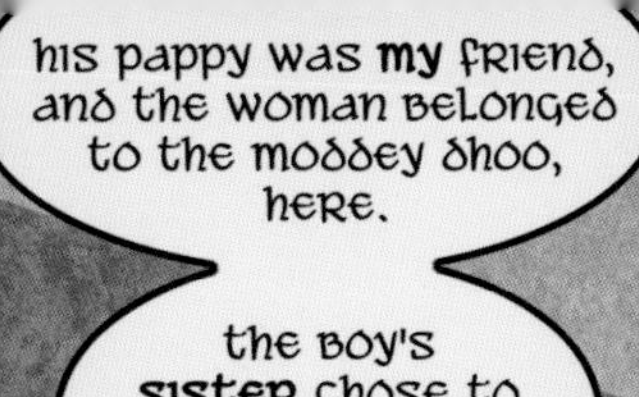
his pappy was **my** friend, and the woman belonged to the moddey dhoo, here.
the boy's **sister** chose to stay beside her mother.
therefore it is only **fair** that the boy himself come with **me**.

OW!

I'll nip yeh harder next time!
hehe!

In this circumstance 'e's allowed ta make a choice, being born of two jurisdictions.

tek'nally, contracts of location and ownership be... uh...

SWISH
ahaha hehe!

she isn't even listening! surma was right, she's too young!
noo! I want to help!
then pay attention! we have arrived.
STORE ROOM

one more thing, pup.

the boy doesn't know he has passed on.

CLICK
passed on what?

SHUFFLE

quick! hide!
what's wrong?
there is a scary witch with a big dog outside my room!
they keep trying to get in.
oh, that's just mathilda and dhoo. they won't hurt you.
they just want to help.
I want to help too.

aahh! What are you doing?!

I'm SORRY!
I don't know what happened!

Get away from me!
Get...
Get away...
Come back!
Wha?!

SHUFFLE
hey, look.
wanna see something cool?

I don't like it.
come on, I think it's great!
CHK CHK!
CHK!
CHOMP

OW! hey!
SMAT

OW OW, JEEZ!
KRIK

oh no
oh no oh no
mum and dad
are gonna be
so mad!
uagh!
make it
stop!

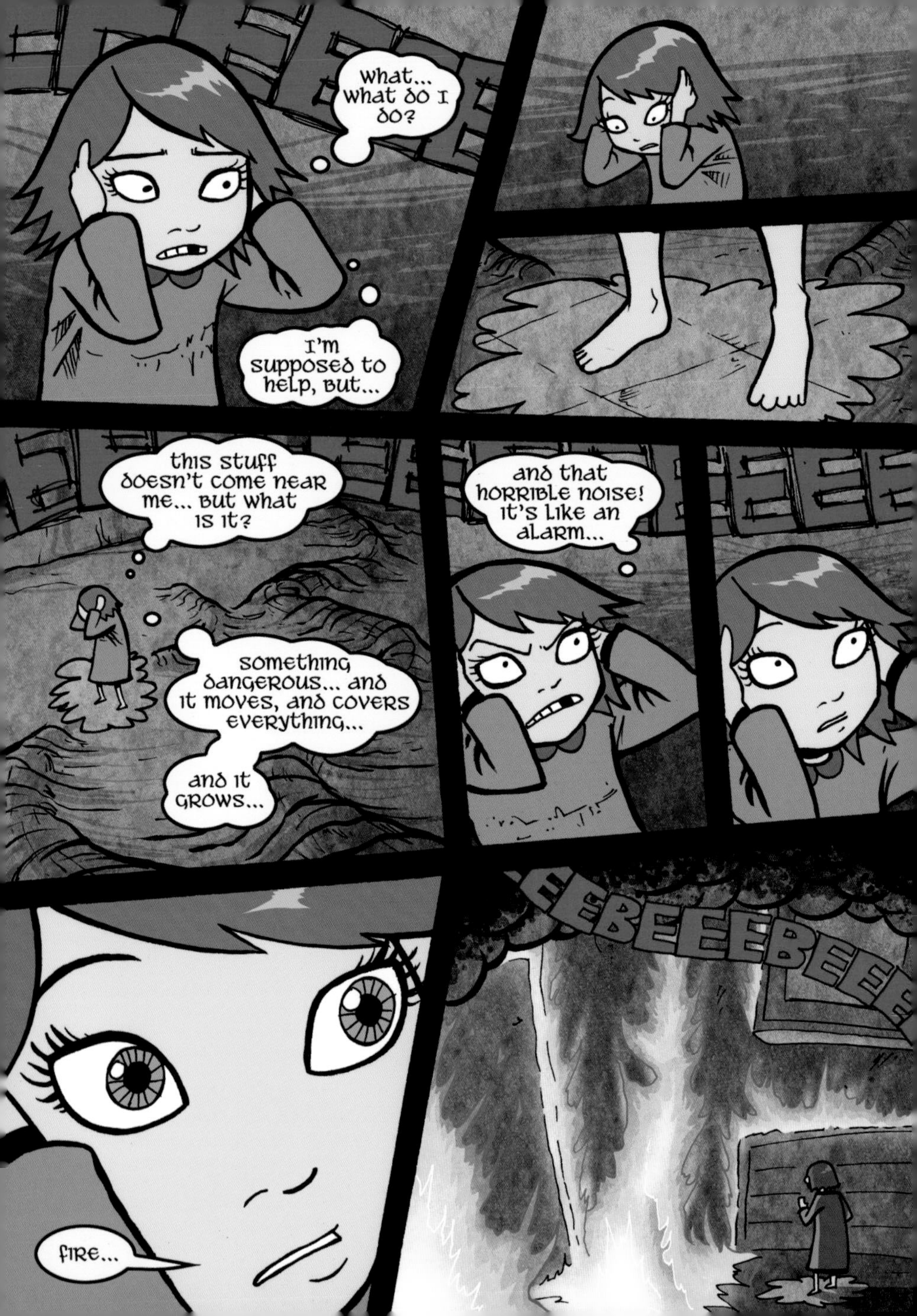
what... what do I do?
I'm supposed to help, but...
this stuff doesn't come near me... but what is it?
something dangerous... and it moves, and covers everything...
and it grows...
and that horrible noise! it's like an alarm...
fire...
EEBEEEBEEE

It's fire! you were playing with fire!
and that noise is a fire alarm!
ahhhh!
nooo!

What do I do what do I do!
always remember one thing...

What did I do?
Something really bad.
But you didn't mean to. It was an accident.
my family ...
I~I think they are with my friends.

well done, child.

martin.
what's done is done.
and now you must choose which of us will take yeh into the **aether**.
SNIFF SNORF

it's okay.

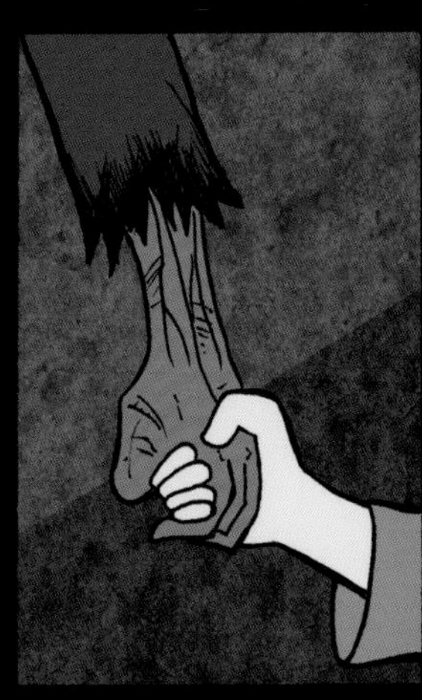

oh my god, annie, that boy burned his house down?
yes. all because he made a mistake.
that's so...
I mean it seems so...
unfair?
the world continues to spin, pup.
the boy and his family will ensure it.
I remember something dhoo told me after he brought me back to my mother.

what does that even mean?
I'm not sure. consolation, perhaps?
implying there is another realm of existence?
maybe it was a reference to this **aether** he mentioned.
this kinda reminds me of the ghost with the sword you met at the **annan waters**.
oh?
yeah, you said your psychopomp friends couldn't help her, right?
so what if she's stuck too?

If that's the case then she might not even know why she is down there.
and she's probably been there a really long time.
It's kinda sad...
I should have tried to help her...
RRP
Instead I was a fool and became scared when I thought she had cut me.
I should have faced my fear, as I did with martin...
What?! come on, she tried to stab you in the face!

say, what did your mum say to you?
how did you know the fire wouldn't hurt you?
it was something I have always kept in mind. she said...
always remember...
remember I will never send you into danger.

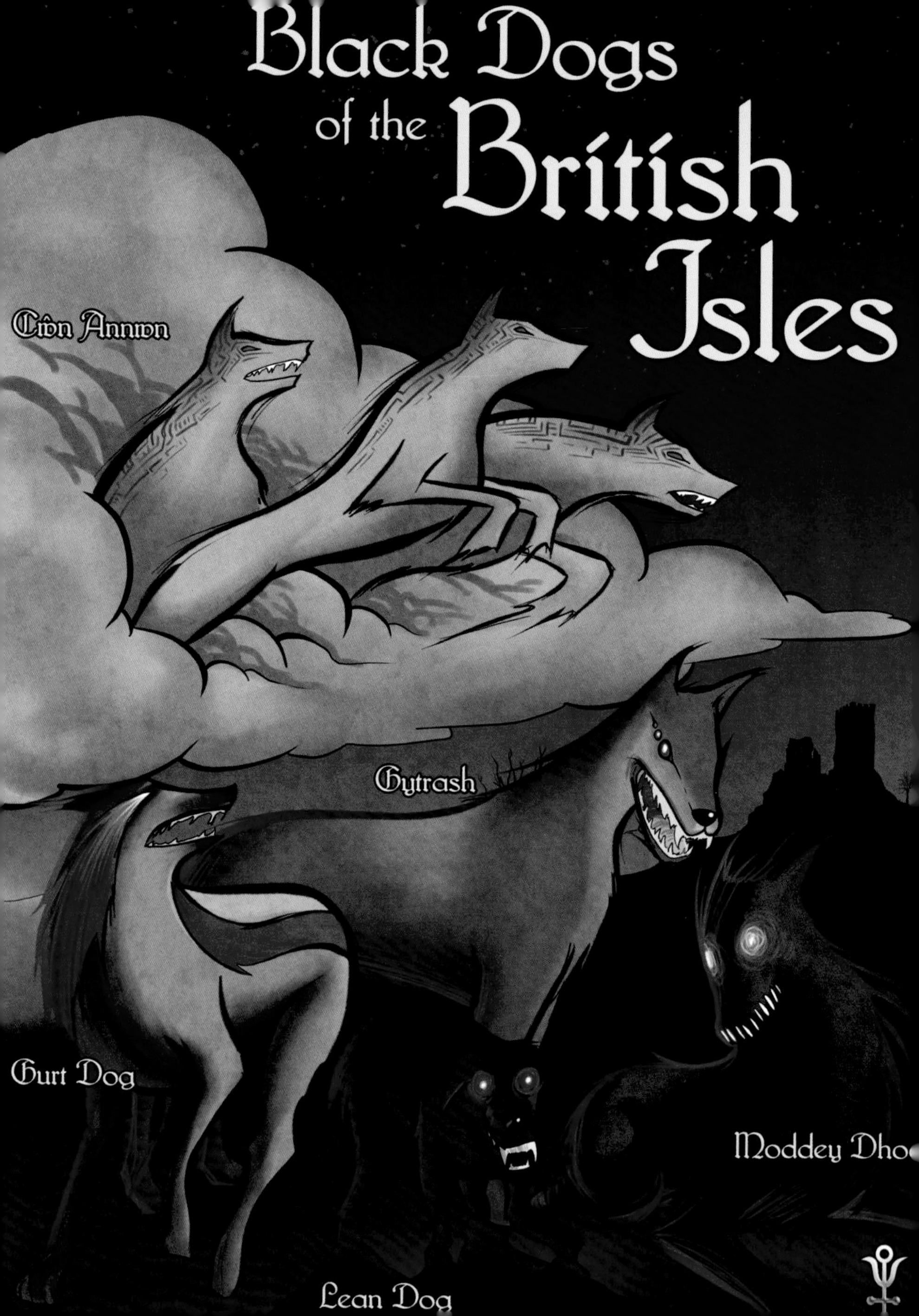
Black Dogs of the British Isles
Cŵn Annwn
Gytrash
Gurt Dog
Moddey Dho
Lean Dog

Gunnerkrigg Court

Chapter 17:

The Medium Beginning

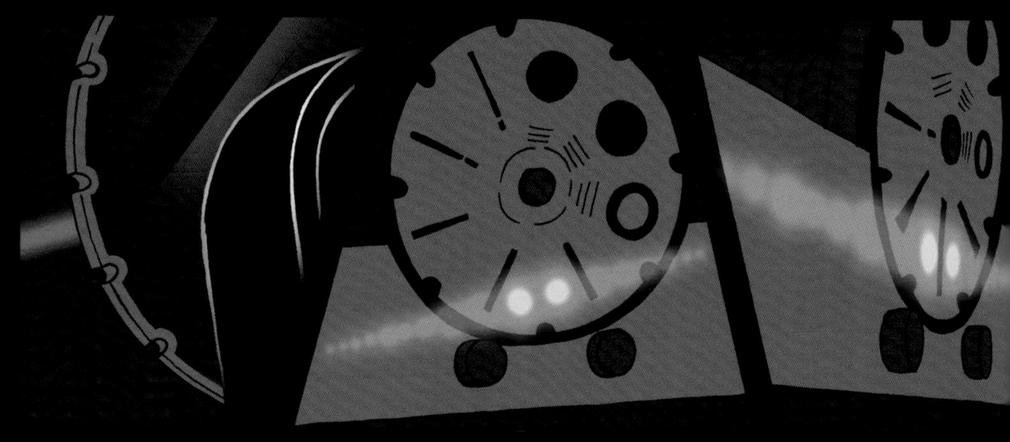

haha, awesome~o!

come on, annie. you don't want to miss the practical!

yes, I'm just going over my answers.

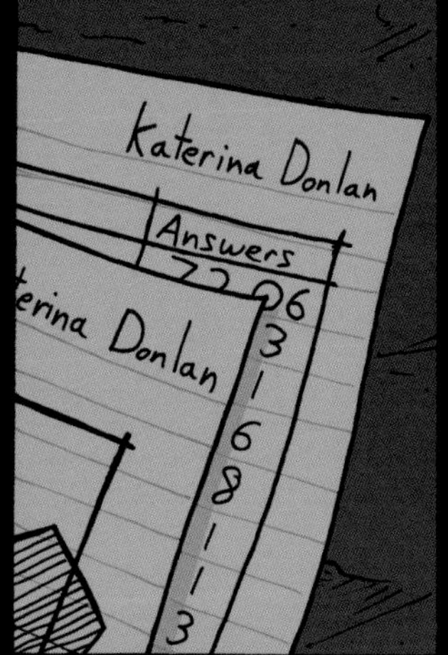
Katerina Donlan
Answers

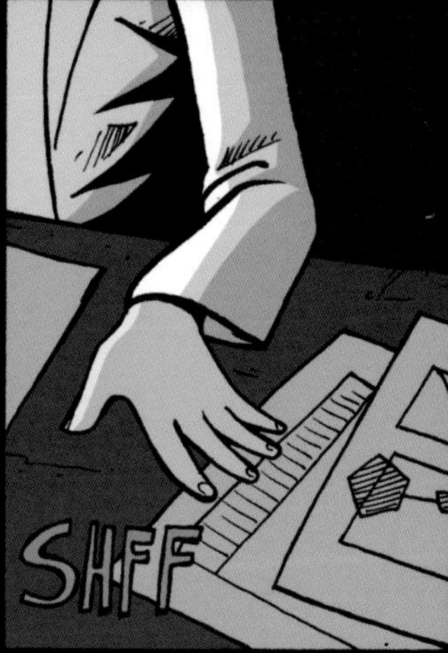
SHFF

SCRIBBLE

COR, LOOK AT HER!
IS SHE A TEACHER?
I DUNNO, MAN, NEVER SEEN HER BEFORE.

collect your things and come with me, please, antimony.

hey, what's going on?

that was miss jones, from the meeting with coyote.

oh, cool! maybe you'll see those older guys again.

perhaps. now, don't get too bored without me.

haha! one does not get "bored" in double physics!
TAP

quite...

miss jones.
just jones will do.

have you given any thought to the headmaster's offer?

yes...
lessons in mediation sound interesting.

very good.
we will begin today.

is this what you teach? how to be a medium?

currently, amongst other things.
2F

Before Coyote left, he said something to you. What was it?
He asked me to visit him in the forest.
He said that? He specifically invited you?
Yes.
Very well, you should take him up on his offer.
He also said I shouldn't trust anyone in the court.
That sounds like something he would say.
Are you going to tell me not to believe his lies?
Coyote is no liar. Therein lies the danger.
Just be careful how you handle his advice.

your mother was the last medium employed by the court.
and the last member of the court allowed into gillitie wood.
I had no idea she worked here. she never mentioned it.
oh? that was your father's influence, I suspect.
yes, he never had patience for matters that didn't fall into a scientific category.
I also hear he has disappeared without a trace.
effectively abandoning you.
it is not a surprise, considering how devoid of emotion he is.
are... are you **trying** to make me angry?
yes.
It helps me assess your character.

parley's lesson is almost over. we will sit and watch.
they teach swordsmanship to the students?
yes. it instills a sense of self awareness and how to read an opponent's body language.
you can soon take stock of a person when you give them a blade.
parley in particular is fairly skilled at **liechtenauer**.
it matches her personality well.

I've noticed an odd duality while I've been at the court.
in the subjects taught, the students, and... **things**... that happen.
for a school of science, there is much that science does not explain.
exactly.
in the glass there. have you ever seen that symbol before?
in many places. my friend kat says it's the alchemical symbol for bismuth.
it serves as a reminder that the court was founded on a union between technological and **etheric** design.
etheric design?
processes unexplained by the science of man.

the court first took root in what was once the heart of gillitie wood.
a group of humans were offered refuge by the creatures of the forest and they worked together to create a place where they could live in peace.
but man's lust for explanation saw him grow tired of etherial tenet.
so concerned were they with the workings of the universe, some of the humans were driven to question their very surroundings.
there was a great division which saw the court and the wood separated.
nature on one side, technology on the other.
and this is where **you** come in.
or people **like** you.

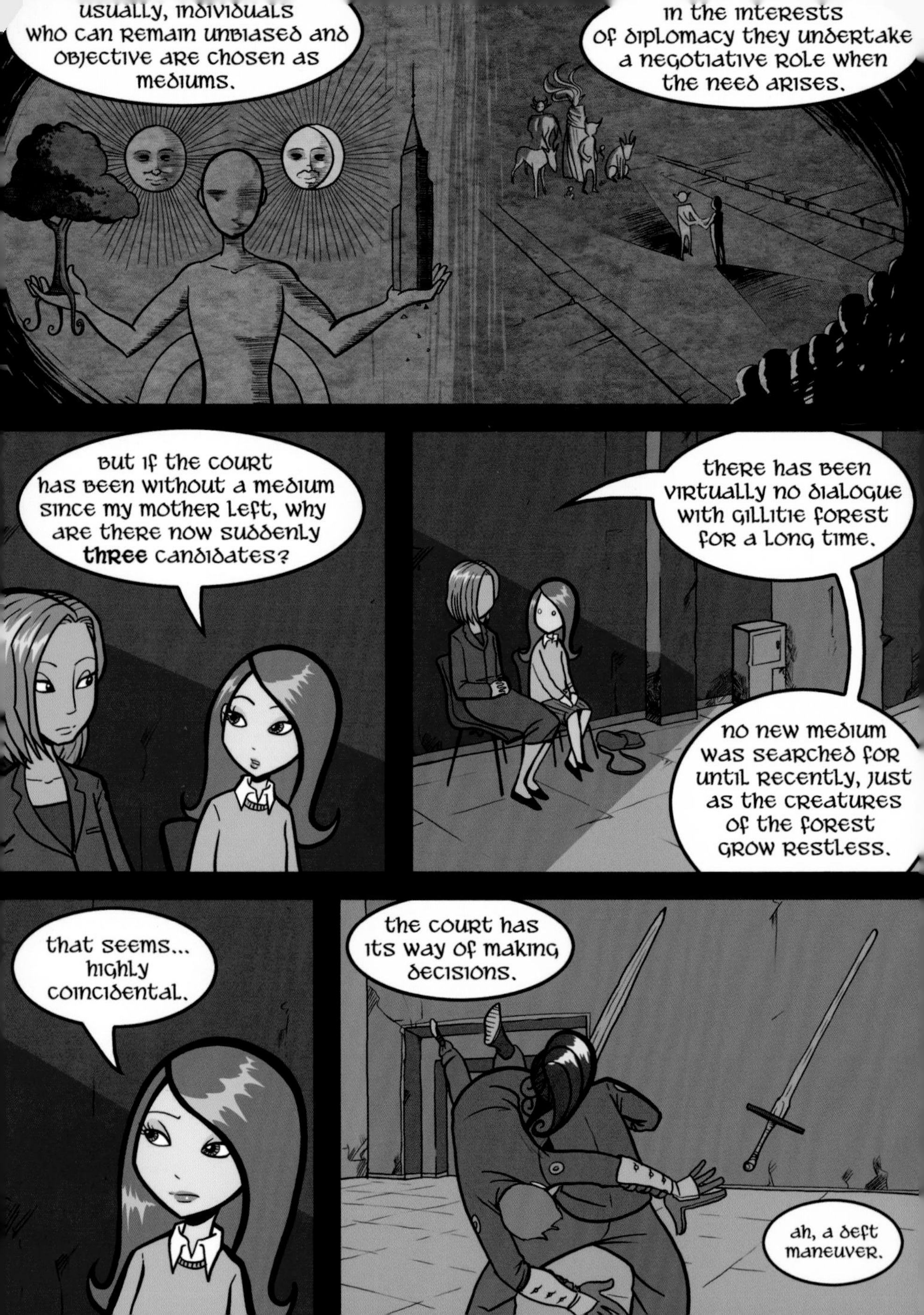
usually, individuals who can remain unbiased and objective are chosen as mediums.
in the interests of diplomacy they undertake a negotiative role when the need arises.
But if the court has been without a medium since my mother left, why are there now suddenly **three** candidates?
there has been virtually no dialogue with gillitie forest for a long time.
no new medium was searched for until recently, just as the creatures of the forest grow restless.
that seems... highly coincidental.
the court has its way of making decisions.
ah, a deft maneuver.

miss jones, I notice you never refer to yourself when talking about the court.
uh... you never say "we" or "us" or "them" when talking about either party.
almost as if you ally yourself with neither side.
a keen observation, antimony.

however, irrelevant.

BRRRING

alright, pack everything away. Let's get a move on.
Growing it out again, James?
heh.
It's been a while.
It has.

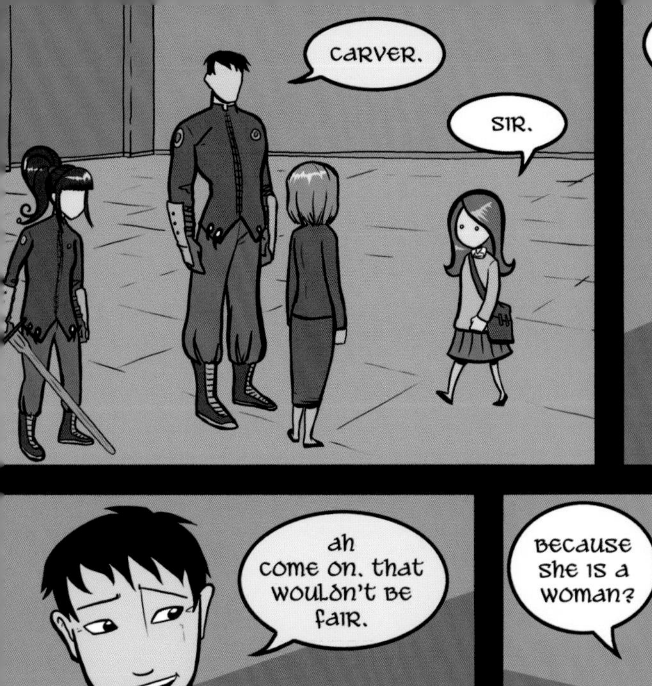
CARVER.
SIR.

here, why don't you an' jones spar? you know, to show carver!

ah come on. that wouldn't be fair.

because she is a woman?

haha! no, because indoors, and at close range, jones would **flatten** me.

oh.

It wouldn't be a real match, James. I can make it quick.
oh snap, SIR! are you gonna take that?!
ahaha! them's fightin' words, Jones!
now I can't refuse!
thank you, parley.
doesn't miss Jones need a sword too?
nah, she never uses 'em.

hey, smitty! just in time, big guy!
hey. hello, carver.
what's going on?
eglamore and jones are having a quickie!
ah. clever.
jeez, eglamore is so **hot!**

huh? **huh?!**

good summer, carver?
yes, thank you.

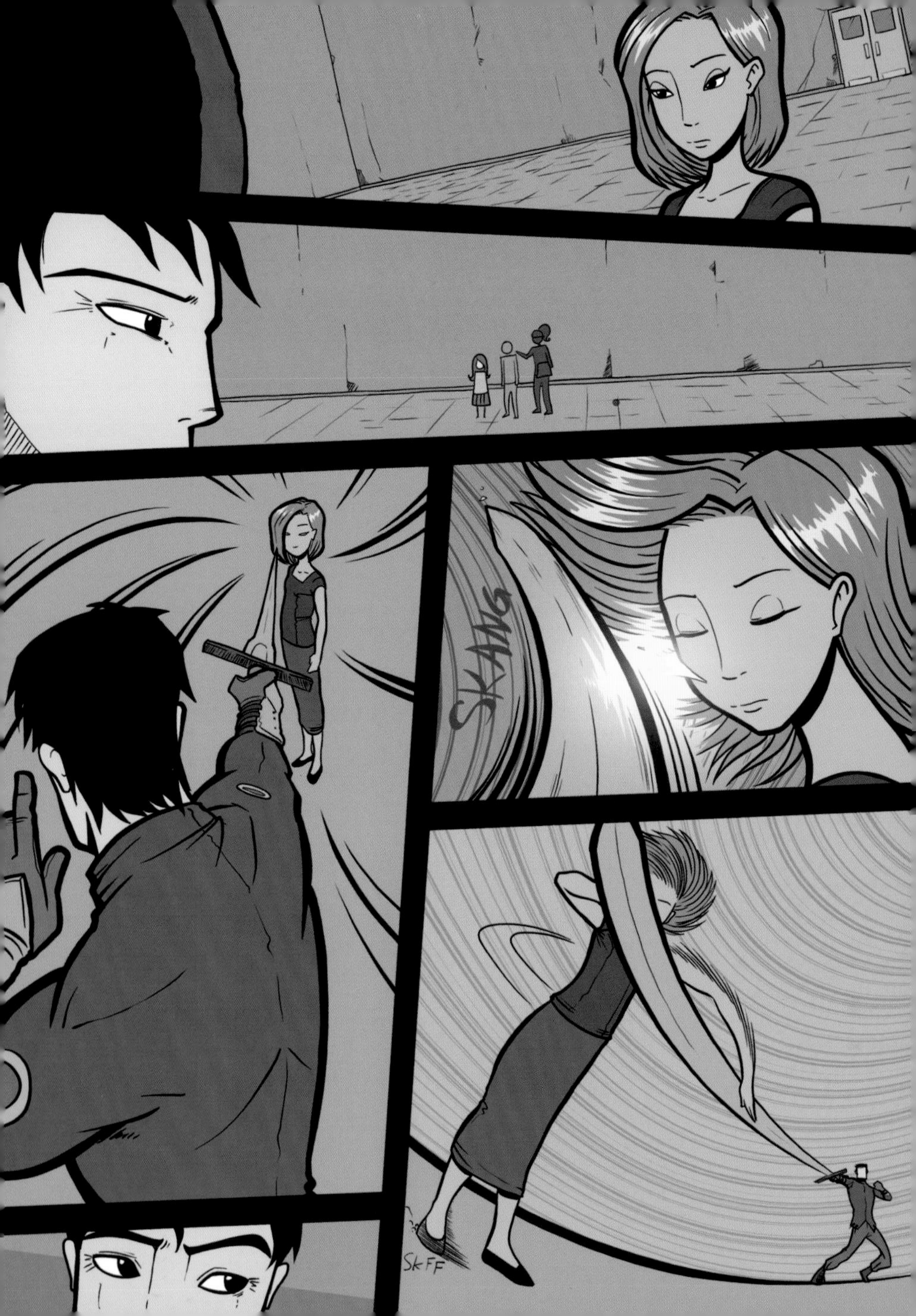
SKANG
SKFF

Right, right, "quick."

damn, you're making me look bad, jo.
your mind is elsewhere, I think, james.
what are you up to? trying to make a point for the carver girl?
"the **carver** girl"?
Is that how you think of her?
you need to watch your step, james.

Grabbing a sword by the blade isn't a valid move, is it?
It is for Jones!
not something you want to try yourself!
and I'm sure the blade glanced her face...
yeah, probably.
Oh damn, here's the next class. I gotta go get changed.
SMACK
try not to get too excited thinking about that, Smits!

and that makes any one of us better suited to mediation than other students?
yes. you may find that many students here have skills whic are **extra normal** in nature.
some of these skills lend themselves well to those in a mediative position.
for example, you have a special empathy with etheric beings, as we saw when you met coyote.
andrew's abilities, on the other hand...
oh hey! I can show you!
I always carry these around so I can show off what he does, haha!

here, g'won!
fling
flip flip flip flip
and look! they're all in order too!
haha! it's like his super power is to make everything **boring**!
it would be more diplomatic to say andrew can subconsciously create order where there was none.

at least I can do something.
hey, shut up, man.
What is it you do, parley?
pfft, my dad is a certified psychic.
parley senior is the only person to have "officially" completed the eugene gould psychic challenge.

that's when they test your psychical ability in a lab.
he won like five million quid cos of it.
put them suckers right outta business!

yeah, he's so good he predicted his son, george would also be psychic.

your first name is george?
s~so what if it is?!
as a prediction, mr. parley filled out a birth certificate for his first born child early.
he got the weight, date, time and everything correct...
everything except the gender.
they fixed her gender, but left her name as george because everyone thought it was hilarious.
wuh~ **you jerk!**

NOD NOD
parley's abilities haven't exactly manifested yet, but chances are good.
she's shown some promise.

now, would any of you care to share your thoughts about the meeting with coyote?
yeah! ysengrin is a huge, angry, jerk. It's obvious that he hates everyone in the court.
coyote seemed very pleased to see the demon, renard. perhaps it was all a ploy to get to him.
um... the headmaster...
be as candid as you wish, antimony.
well... the headmaster was acting very rudely.
he didn't seem to care at all about the meeting.
yes, very good. that's exactly the sort of observation you'll need to keep in mind.

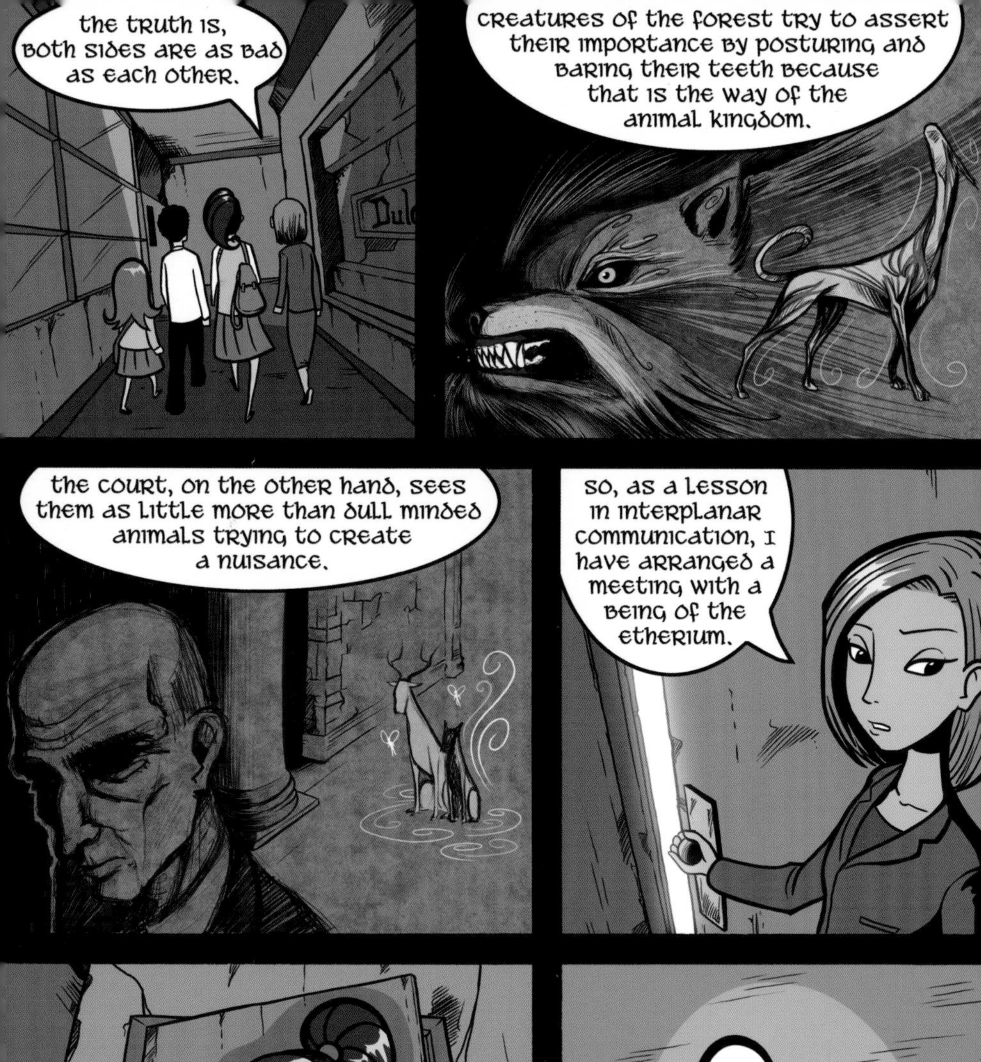
the truth is, both sides are as bad as each other.
creatures of the forest try to assert their importance by posturing and baring their teeth because that is the way of the animal kingdom.
the court, on the other hand, sees them as little more than dull minded animals trying to create a nuisance.
so, as a lesson in interplanar communication, I have arranged a meeting with a being of the etherium.

wow, a ghost!
spectral being!
do you mean us harm?!
we wish to communicate with you!

annie, why is she talking like that?
I...
I'm not really sure.

What?!
antimony, you know this boy?
yes. he is a friend of mine. his name is mort.
mort, this is andrew smith.
alright.
alright, mate.
and this is... um, parley.
GREETINGS HUMAN PERSON!
yeah, I'm laffin'.

so you're a ghost, huh? what do you do?
well, I scare people. it's all very important, I assure you.
you know, when I first met annie she gave me some advice.
advice like what?
like... to be more subtle.
subtle? what's that got to do with...
hwaaah!
haw!

ahahaha! what else can you do?!
oh, all sorts of stuff!
Silenti
it depends on the situation, see...

thank you again, mortimer.
no problem, jones.
alright, see ya.
alright, mate, see ya.
FAREWELL hahaha!
kat and I will stop by soon, mort.
shucks, that'd be neat.

ah! time to eat! let's go get something.
I'm not really hungry.
yeah y'are. come on.

well done, antimony.
through you, parley, andrew and mortimer were able to get along amicably.
but I already knew mort. I don't think it counts.
the fact you were able to befriend him on your own certainly does count.
the next time might not be so easy, but it was a good first step, I feel.
when you want to go into the forest let me know.
Sil
w-when will I be ready?
while I will continue to instruct you, I will not be making your decisions.
I leave the choice up to you.

If coyote promised no harm would come to you, you can be certain he will make sure of it.
it should only be a casual meeting anyway, and it will do you good to hear their side of the story.
until then you will have lessons with parley and andrew each week.
goodbye.
you shouldn't eavesdrop, mort.
ahh! how did you know?!

SWORDS

Gunnerkrigg Court

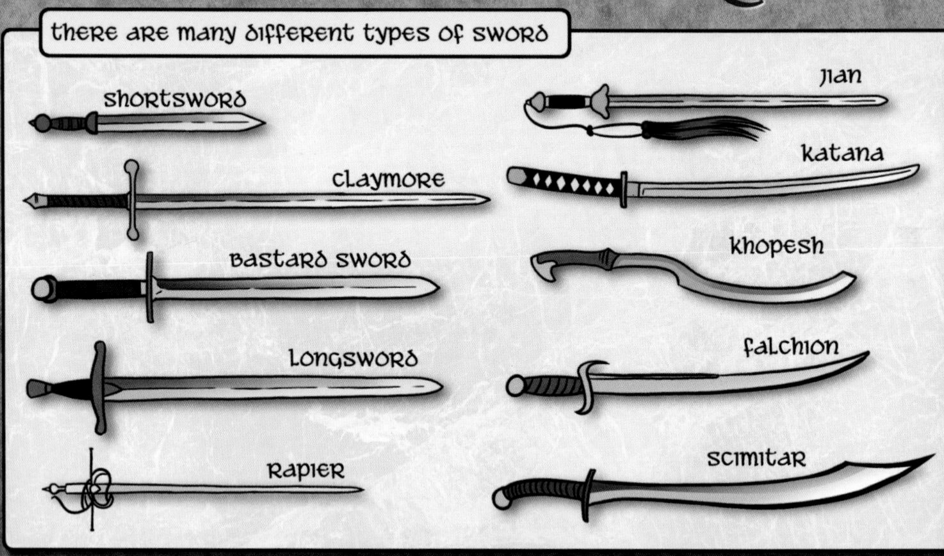
there are many different types of sword
shortsword
claymore
bastard sword
longsword
rapier
jian
katana
khopesh
falchion
scimitar

anatomy of a sword:
hilt
pommel
grip
cross guard
rain guard
blade
fuller
edge
central ridge
point
I think swords are neat do you think swords are neat!!
a sword is a tool designed to inflict pain or death on a fellow human!
often spiritualised and glorified, they also serve as a physical metaphor for humanity's eternal, savage thirst for destruction!

Gunnerkrigg Court

Chapter 18:

S1

uh oh, watch out.

What, who is she?
She's in our class, right?

her mom is our form teacher, and I heard her dad is a teacher too!

ugh, **both** her parents are teachers? she could get us into trouble like whenever.

hi guys!
some first day, huh?!
wanna get something to eat?

I know where the canteen...

huh!
Real slick, Donlan.

hi, mum!
hi, dad!
katja! antimony!
hello!
I was
wonderin' if
you guys...

waaait... what's
going on here?
nothing!

I uh... was wondering
if you knew someplace
I could use as a
workshop.
I
wanna try
building a
robot.

oh... a~a ROBOT?
well, give me a moment.
so! outgrown the science labs already, eh?
yeah. It's annoying that I can't leave the labs set up how I want.
here we are.
this key unlocks my old unit down by the west canals. It's empty now, but there is plenty of space.

th~the address is on the keyring. it's not hard to get to.
that's perfect! thanks, mum!

Oh... I WISH I COULD GO WITH THEM...
YOU COULD ALWAYS ASK...
NO...
NO... LET THEM FIGURE IT OUT.
OUR TIME HAS PASSED.
WELL, I THINK THERE IS SOME LIFE LEFT IN US YET.

yeah, I guess you could say I've known him my whole life.
Of course, he was uncle jimmy before he was mister eglamore.

uncle jimmy?

haha! I know, Right?

has he...
GOONIES
has he ever mentioned a woman?

huh... you know, I don't think he has...
MP3

I don't remember him **ever** saying anything about a girlfriend, or a lady he likes or anything.

I think there might be something going on between him and miss jones.

ha! there better not be, or I'd have to beat her up!

you might have some trouble there, dearest, you see, I also think Jones is a robot.
Whaaaa...
come on! first off, a human looking robot is called an "android"
and second, there is no way you could make an android that looks that good.
we have seen stranger.
remember that cursed teapot?
yeahhhhh... but that was...
I don't even know what that was about...
but a totally human looking android...
nah...
just... nah.
Scratch
you're thinkin about makin one, aren't you?

A*
Excellent!

hey, what'd you get?

is this one of those situations where you pretend to be interested and then throw it back in my face?
like those other times?

whaat?!
she got an a **star**!

of course she did! her parents helped her!
this was really hard!
...no fair!
...she always...

...stayed up all night...
...always showing off...

the human body is essentially a biological machine. It relies on contractile tissue for movement.
most of our robots have ultra high torque actuators in their joints. that's how they move.
so their point of locomotion is in their joints? that's not quite how muscles work.
haw! look at that!
hey! nice teddy!
Born To Heckle
are you off to nursery?
well, maybe hydraulics are closer to how... how a muscle...
hey you!
carrot top!
are you okay, kat?
those guys over there are being jerks.
hey! shut up!
ooooo!
haha!

Bah. those Buffoons!
Insult you, would they...
perhaps you might scare them away for us.
!
my pleasure!
araRaRaRaRaRaRaR!
are you allowed to let him do that?!
ahhh!
I absolutely did not expect thiiiis!
Oh, I sincerely doubt it.

ahahaha! how hilarious it is to watch humans running!
TROT
why thank you, Reynardine.
and I didn't even have to issue you a command.
well...
one is allowed to defend one's own honour.
train's here.

ROBOT!
mu...annie! kat!
did you find the place okay?
yes! shadow 2 is already inside.
ZZZIP
there is nobody around for quite a way. the place is fairly deserted.
just like the rest of the court, then.
hahaa! check this out this is awesome!
yay!

not many people would get excited by a large, empty room.
It may be empty but it's **full** of potential!
Robot, I'm gonna make you the **best** new body!
ah! thank you so much!
hey, look what I found over here.

huh! mum didn't give me a key for this.
perhaps Reynardine...

could smash the lock!

could pick the lock properly
aw.

tension wrench, rake, then diamond, just as I showed you.
RAS
RAS

haha! watch, as human technology crumbles before me!

hmm, an ominous passage that plunges into an inky blackness, sealed behind lock and chain.
you know what this means.

we must see where it leads!
damn straight!

It wasn't so hard. you see, the key was to remain focused.
that's pretty neat, Reynardine.

looks like it keeps on going down.
and I didn't bring a light.

perhaps we can use this...
FWOOSH

you gotta let me examine that thing one day, annie. figure out how it burns some things and not others.

It behaves that way because she wills it so.
that's how a blinker stone works!

that doesn't explain anything!
it explains **enough**, doesn't it?
ugh! that's a terrible ethic!

I felt around a little and it looks like the coast is clear.
thank you, shadow 2.

soon.
oh, we got to the bottom, finally.

this room must be very large. I can't see the walls or the ceiling.

I saw a plug on the end of this cable near the entrance. maybe it leads to...

ah yes, a flood light.
I guess my mum set these up when she still worked here.

If you stay here with Reynardine and Robot, Shadow 2 and I will nip back and plug them in.

won't be long!

heyyy Ren~ar~deeen!
what is it?
that was pretty cute how you got all defensive about annie before.
you were all "insult you would they?!"
wh... no I wasn't! I said "us."
insult us, would they
no you didn't
yes I did!
hehe, okay then. whatever you say.
...
you are a good friend to her, katerina.
huh?
how is she doing in her studies?
does she have many other friends?
has anyone been giving her trouble?
has a boy caught her eye?

woah woah, where did all this come from? are you like her dad in disguise now?

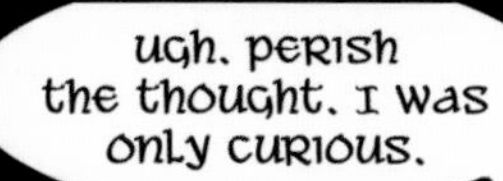
ugh. perish the thought. I was only curious.

I assumed you would know her best, since you spend so much time together.
all she talks about is you.

this is a set up for another lewd joke, isn't it? what do **you** care?

forget it.
huh! you're being serious aren't you?

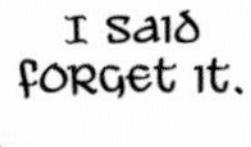
I said forget it.

you should stay as a wolf more often, dude. you're much nicer this way.
well, the mind is nothing but a plaything of the body, correct?

wha?
CHACK

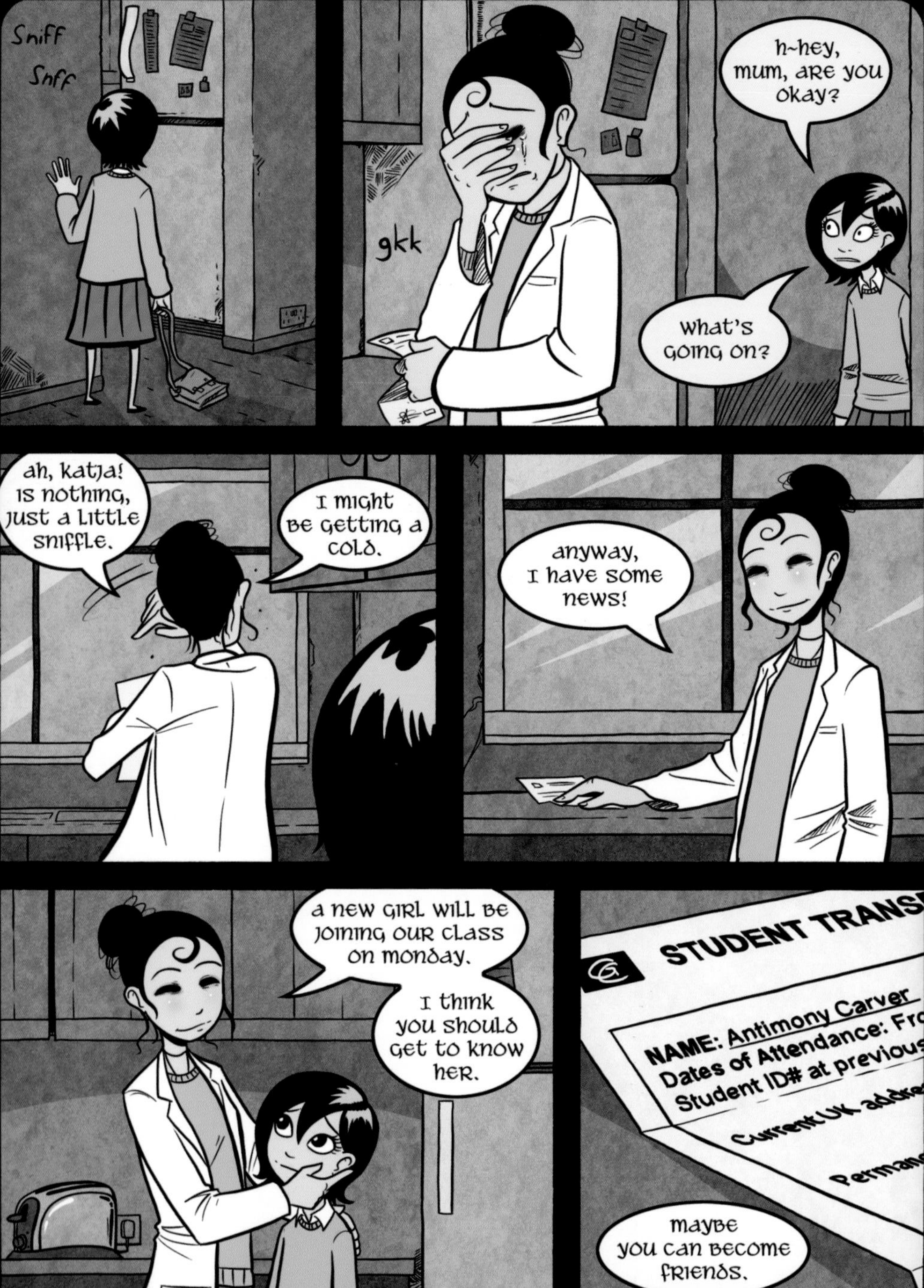
Sniff
Snff
gkk
h-hey, mum, are you okay?
What's going on?
ah, katja! is nothing, just a little sniffle.
I might be getting a cold.
anyway, I have some news!
a new girl will be joining our class on monday.
I think you should get to know her.
STUDENT TRANS
NAME: Antimony Carver
Dates of Attendance: Fr
Student ID# at previous
Current UK addre
Perman
maybe you can become friends.

aIIIEEEEEE!
kat!
kat are you okay what happened?!
hahaha!
look at 'em all!
have you ever seen anything like it?!

I've **never** seen robots as elaborate as these before!
they're gorgeous!
some of them even look like they might be early designs for existing models.
here's an **h model**, but look how super fancy it is!
and the hands on this one are so delicate!

and this one...

maybe we can put a blanket over it.

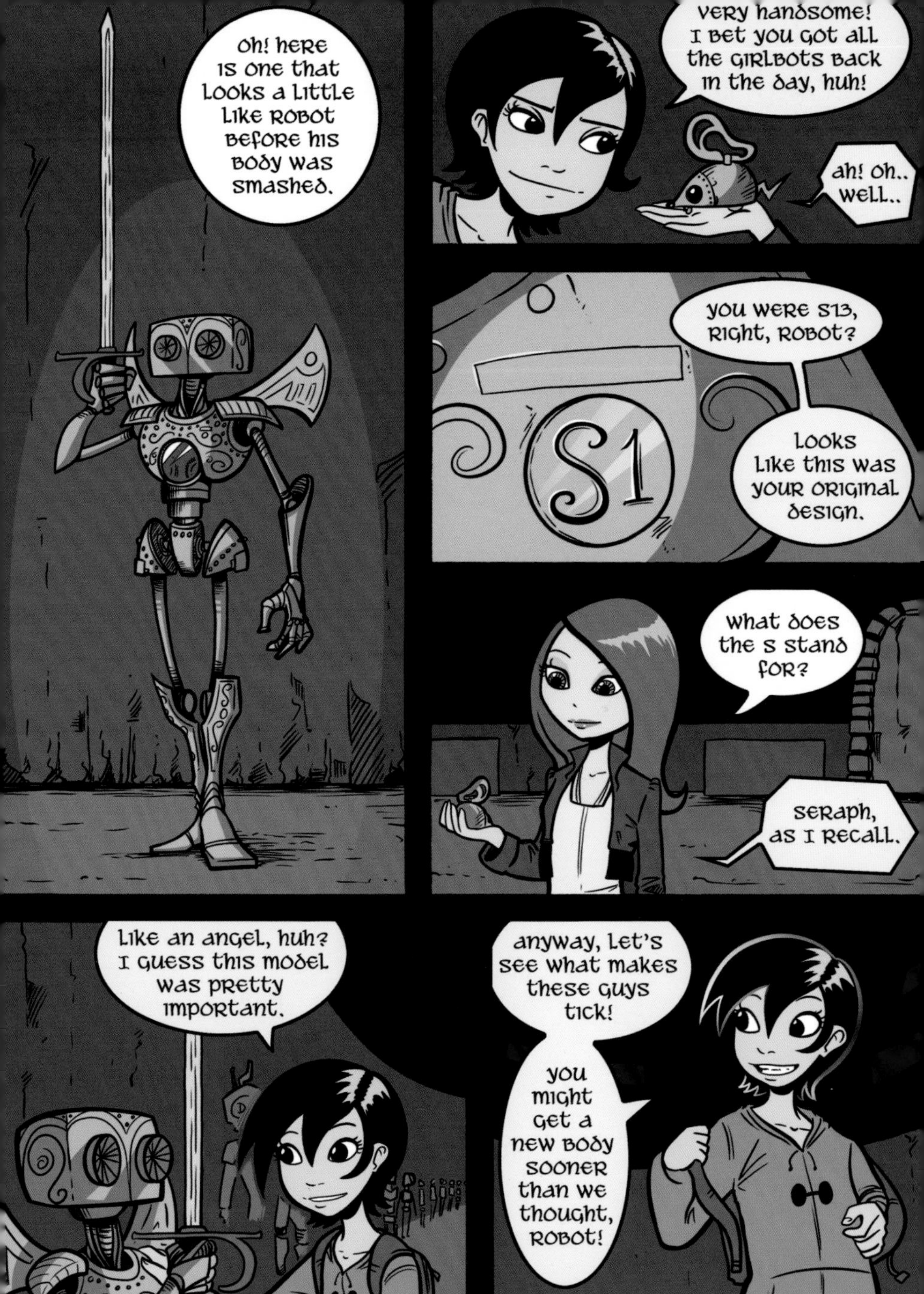
Oh! here is one that looks a little like Robot before his body was smashed.
Very handsome! I bet you got all the girlbots back in the day, huh!
ah! oh.. well..
You were S13, right, Robot?
Looks like this was your original design.
S1
What does the S stand for?
Seraph, as I recall.
Like an angel, huh? I guess this model was pretty important.
Anyway, let's see what makes these guys tick!
You might get a new body sooner than we thought, Robot!

SKITTER
haha! whooo!
ZZZZIP!
Sniff
no!
no no no!
useless! they're all useless!
there's no drive system!
no kinetic alternator!
there isn't even a power source!
there are no electrically driven components at all!
all these beautiful, mechanically sound machines, and they don't do anything!

how disappointing...
my mum must have realised they were useless too and left them down here.
wonder who made them...

perhaps they work through means you are unfamiliar with?
you should try robot's cpu in one of them.

it wouldn't work. I mean, there's a cpu slot, but no power or anything.

you made robot in year 7, right? so you can see these are pretty much just giant, poseable action figures.

actually, all I did was put his limbs and head on to his body and switch him on.
I don't have the first idea how to make a robot.

SEE? NOTHING.
CLANG

WHAT IF YOU TRIED IT IN HIS ORIGINAL DESIGN?

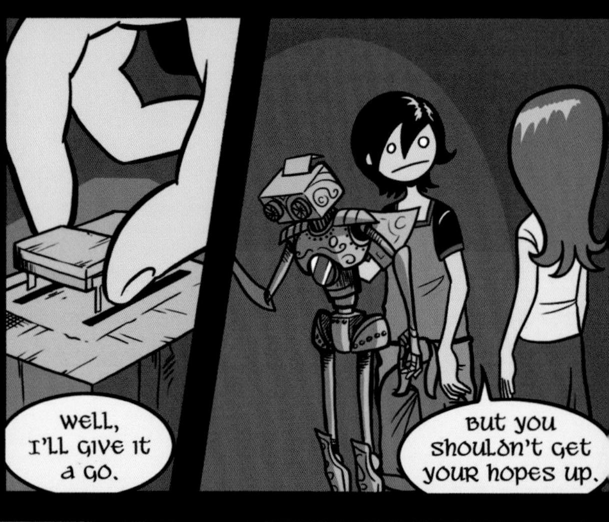
WELL, I'LL GIVE IT A GO.
BUT YOU SHOULDN'T GET YOUR HOPES UP.

SNAP

JEANNE!

kat, I think something's WRONG with him!

I'll say! he's Runnin' around when he shouldn't be!
CLANK

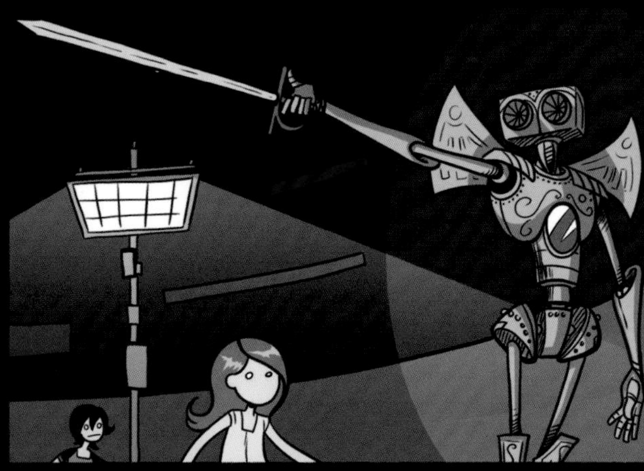

ROBOT?
ROBOT, WHO IS JEANNE?

HOOOOOH
she died and we did nothing.

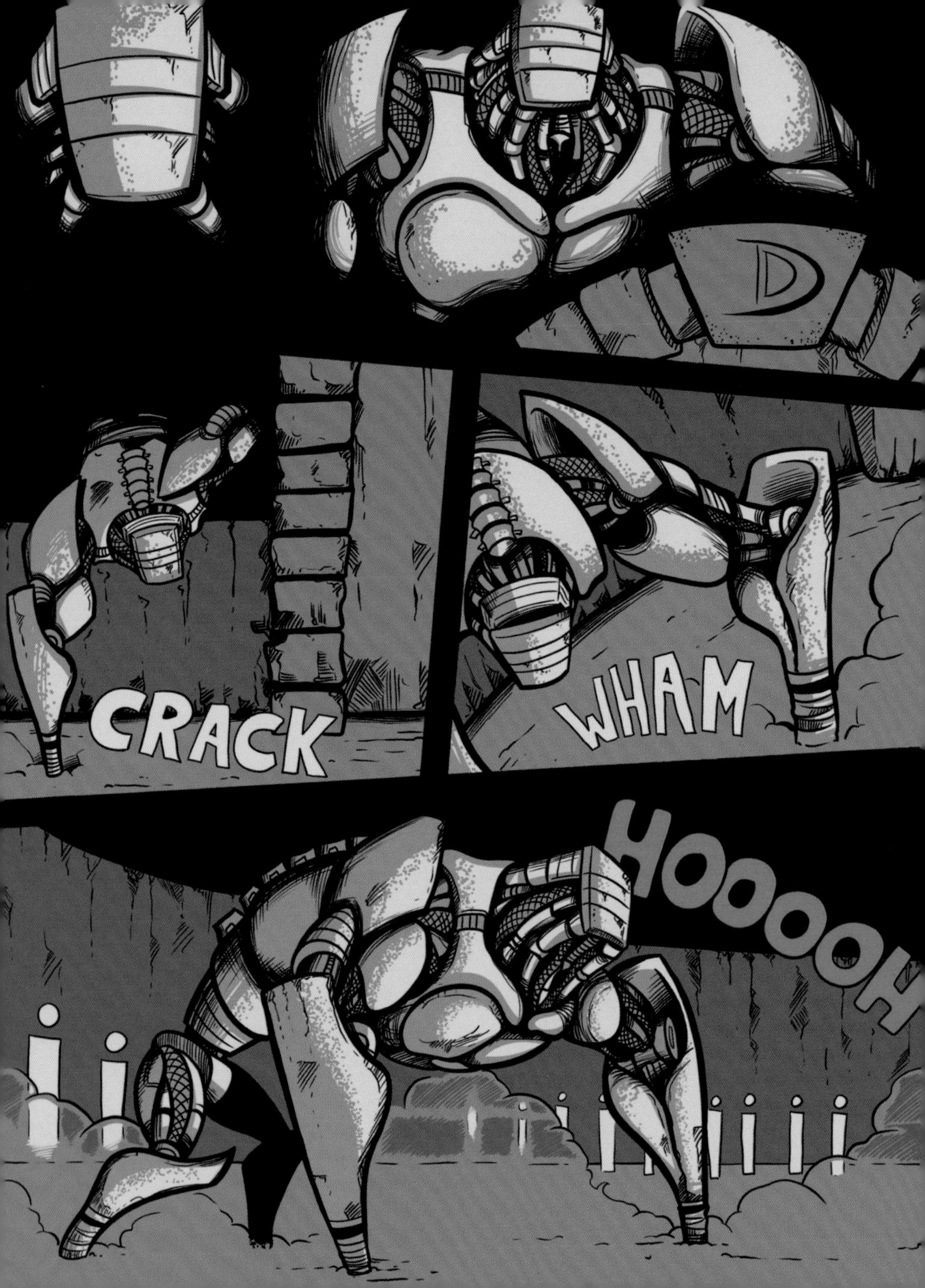
CRACK
WHAM
HOOOOOH
¡¡¡¡¡¡¡¡

Get Back!
Get Back you two!
hey! watch it, Buddy!
BUMP
What IS that thing?!
HOOOOOOH
THUD
THUD
THUD
THUD
THUD
WHUD

you will pay for what you did to her.
but you will never be forgiven.
WRR
CHACK
HOOOOOOOH
CLANG
TING
KANG
SNICK

SHHP
THOK
THOK
THOK
THOK
THOK
SWIT
SWIT
SWIT

I dunno what's goin' on, but this isn't a fair fight.
you noticed it too?
noticed what?
this so called "fight" is scripted.
CHACK
a morbid play acted out by thes machines.

ZASH

CLAP
CLAP

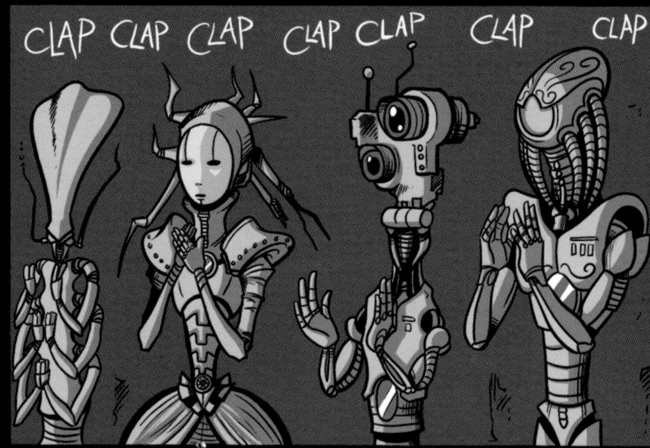
CLAP CLAP CLAP CLAP CLAP CLAP CLAP

now they're all moving!

CLAP
CLAP
CLAP
CLAP
CLAP

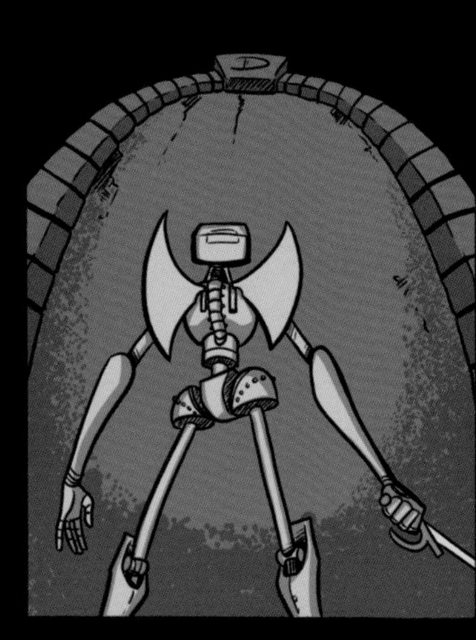

SLASH

WHAM

he's going into that hole!

Let's follow him.

hang on, let me get Robot's mouse body.

there's a light up ahead...

z z z z z z z z z z z z

It's her.
Jeanne is the ghost by the annan waters.

annie, she's beautiful!
her features have withered over time, but it's definitely her.
this must be the guy that made the robots. "diego".
Diego
a coward's shrine. made in tribute to a woman he loved from afar.
I didn't take you for an expert on the human condition, Reynardine.
we know nothing of this diego.
perhaps not, but do you think a woman like that could ever feel anything other than pity for such a runt of a man?
o~oh my god! that's the worst thing in the world to say!
ah, then I must be mistaken, I'm sure.

what else can you tell us?
well, you see how uneasy the girl is in her finery.
how she clutches the sword in comfort.
a soldier perhaps?
and the mechanical monster outside.
a representation of someone involved in her death?
for all his technical wonders, this diego was unable to save her.
so he fabricated this contrivance, this fantasy of his, and squirreled it away beneath the ground.
look well, girls.
know that this is all that is left of a man's heart.
this tiny, stone room.

you called him a coward.

he admitted as much himself.

when you asked this contraption "who is jeanne?" it replied...
she died and we did nothing.

hey, see if Robot is okay!
oh yeah.
anyway, you make this guy sound kinda crummy, Reynardine.
what if... Jeanne's ghost is by the river, right? what if she died by falling off the bridge?
and Diego made those robot birds to save anyone else who falls!
so he did some good!

he might have even saved your life, annie!

I'm not sure. If she died in a simple accident, why is she still down there?
JOE COOL

maybe everything that dies down there has to stay?
But those fairies...

hey, you okay in there?
Tappy Tap

I... that monster out there. I had such a hatred for it I could not...

ah...
what a beautiful lady.

say, robot, who looks after you guys? like, who fixes you when you break?
nobody.
the court robots have always maintained themselves.

huh! I guess when diego died you couldn't make more of yourselves, so you changed to simpler designs.
and these old models are so complex I can't figure them out.
one thing's for sure; these things don't use servos or hydraulics or anything like that.

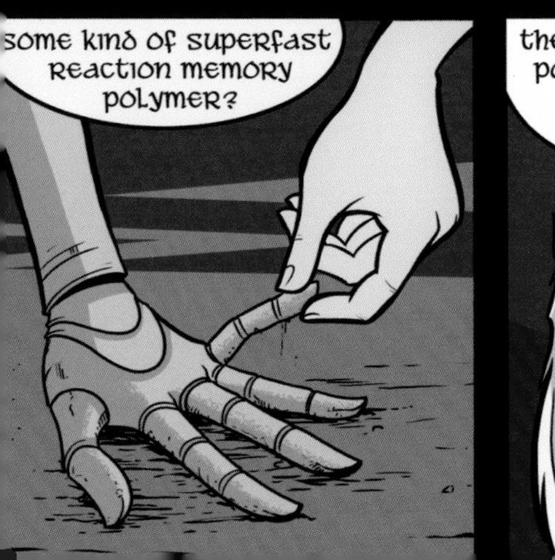
some kind of superfast reaction memory polymer?

they could be powered by etheric means.

you mean like **magic**?
come on, man, just because something isn't explained yet doesn't make it magic.

anyway I know I'll figure it out eventually!
CRACK
thank you for your help, kat. we couldn't do any of this without you.
now we know jeanne's name.
yeah! thanks kat!
thank you!
aw I didn't do anything. we work together, right?
we all chipped in.
even you, moody.
har har.

and now we have a place to work, we can **really** get started on a new body for robot!

so I was thinking more about androids...

not likely, miss! she's always swotting in the **study hall.** **hahaha!**

...

heh.

BRRING

antimony!
wait for me!

CLICK
ah, I think I never get it!
just to get one of those robots to move. I wish I could see it!
you'll figure it out, anny.
is strange. such similar designs to certain court robots, but the technology is very different.
what do you think?
yikes! don't ask me! I'm two short planks compared to you.
oh now! you and me are smart on different things! and when we work together, we are unstoppable!

's so sad. all those figures standing there. like they waiting for something.
yeah...
and you are waiting too. you miss him.
yeah yeah. 'im and 'is stupid training.
he's away so offen.
he does it for you, you know.
he doesn't hafta do anything.
just be here.
'sides, sometimes I think donny misses jim more than I do.
hahaha! those boys, always so close! I think you might be right!

Gunnerkrigg Court

Gunnerkrigg Court

Chapter 19:

Power Station

there's no need to worry, kat. you and I have snuck out before.
yeah but now there will be **boys** there!

you see the boys almost every day in class.

I know I know, but this is different... seeing them after we should be in bed and all...

we don't have to go if you don't want.

no, no, this has been planned for ages, and I can get us all past the security system.
I mean that's the only reason we were invited, right?

Reynardine tried to insist on being a chaperone when he heard some of the boys would be there.
ahaha! aww, really? he can be pretty sweet sometimes. he's just a big ol' softie, isn't he?
oh yeah...
a big old softie that tried to kill me, yes.
TAP
TAP-TAP
there's the signal.
let's do this!

hey, all set?
yeah.
then let us away.
EXIT
SCHEDULE

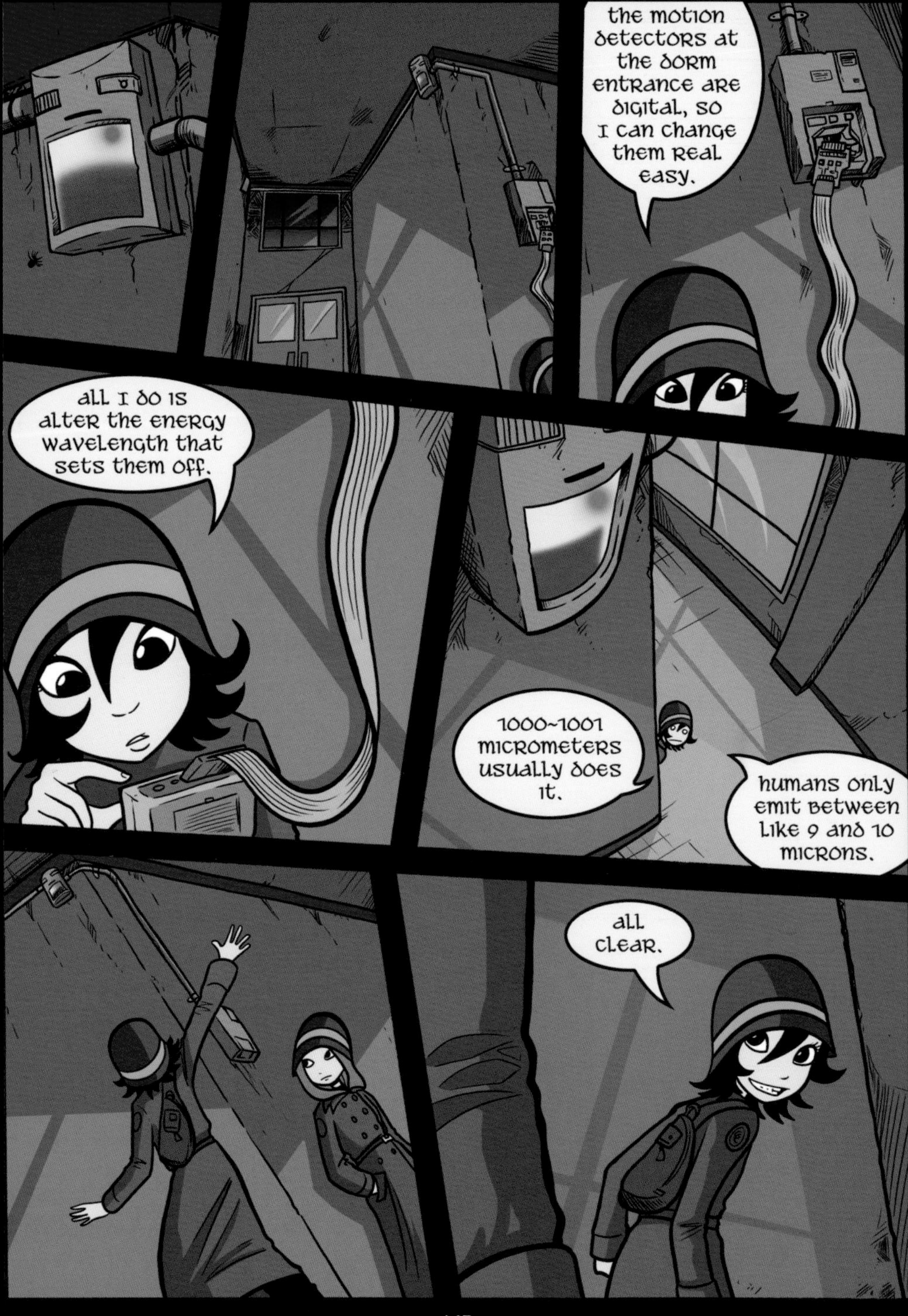
the motion detectors at the dorm entrance are digital, so I can change them real easy.
all I do is alter the energy wavelength that sets them off.
1000~1001 micrometers usually does it.
humans only emit between like 9 and 10 microns.
all clear.

ROOF
ACCESS

hey, you made it.
I'm sure there was never a doubt.

hi, John.
h-hi, margo.
easy now, Romeo.
shut it, matt.

this here is jack, from qs. he found it.
aright.
so where is it?
ROOF ACCESS
Right this way.

CLANG
CLANG
CLANG
there's a wall around the whole compound.
this building has the best view cos it's right next to the artifical lake.
What are they doing over there?
they're gearin' up for an experiment.
what kind of experiment?
you'll know as much as I do when you see it.

so how did you find this place, Jack?
aw, there's way too much stuff to see around the court.
I go out exploring all the time.
I just fiddle with the dorm's motion detectors and it's easy to slip away.
hey, that's what I did too.
Oh aye?
wow, I'm surprised you guys aren't fighting.
differences can be set aside for one evening, I think.
yeah, I'm cool.

SO, KAT, YOU'RE NOT GOING TO BE TELLING YOUR MUM AND DAD ABOUT THIS, ARE YOU?

JEEZ, WILLIE, WHY WOULD I WANT TO DO THAT?
I'D GET IN TROUBLE TOO.
YEAH MAN, BESIDES, DON'T FORGET WHO JANET'S DAD IS.
THEREFORE, I RECOMMEND REMAINING SQUARELY IN MY GOOD BOOKS.
OOF! HA!

CLONK
WHAM
HUH?
OH NO!
HUF!
BLOOMIN' DOOR.
GOD DAMMIT.
DAMN IIIIT!

hey!
uh...

they're what?!

ger off don't touch 'er what are you doin' I~I'll bust you up real bad!

zimmy...
carver! what's goin' on?! I thought it wuz night time!
it is. we came to look at the power station.

yuh... yer not uspposed to be up at night! I's allowed but you en't!
I could get you all in big trouble if you try anyfing!
hey!
what?!
no no, it's okay, zimmy, nobody is going to try anything...

cześć, annie.
cześć, gamma.
why are you here, zimmy?
that... fing out there. It's screwin' with my head. finally found it.

hi, are you in year 9? I like your hair.

gamma doesn't speak english.
oh...

she's 14 but still in year 8 like us, you got a problem with that?!
!

ugh, don't worry about it, margo. zimmy's always like this.

<do...do they all think I am stupid and ugly?>

<no, why you think that?>

<zimmy translates for me.>

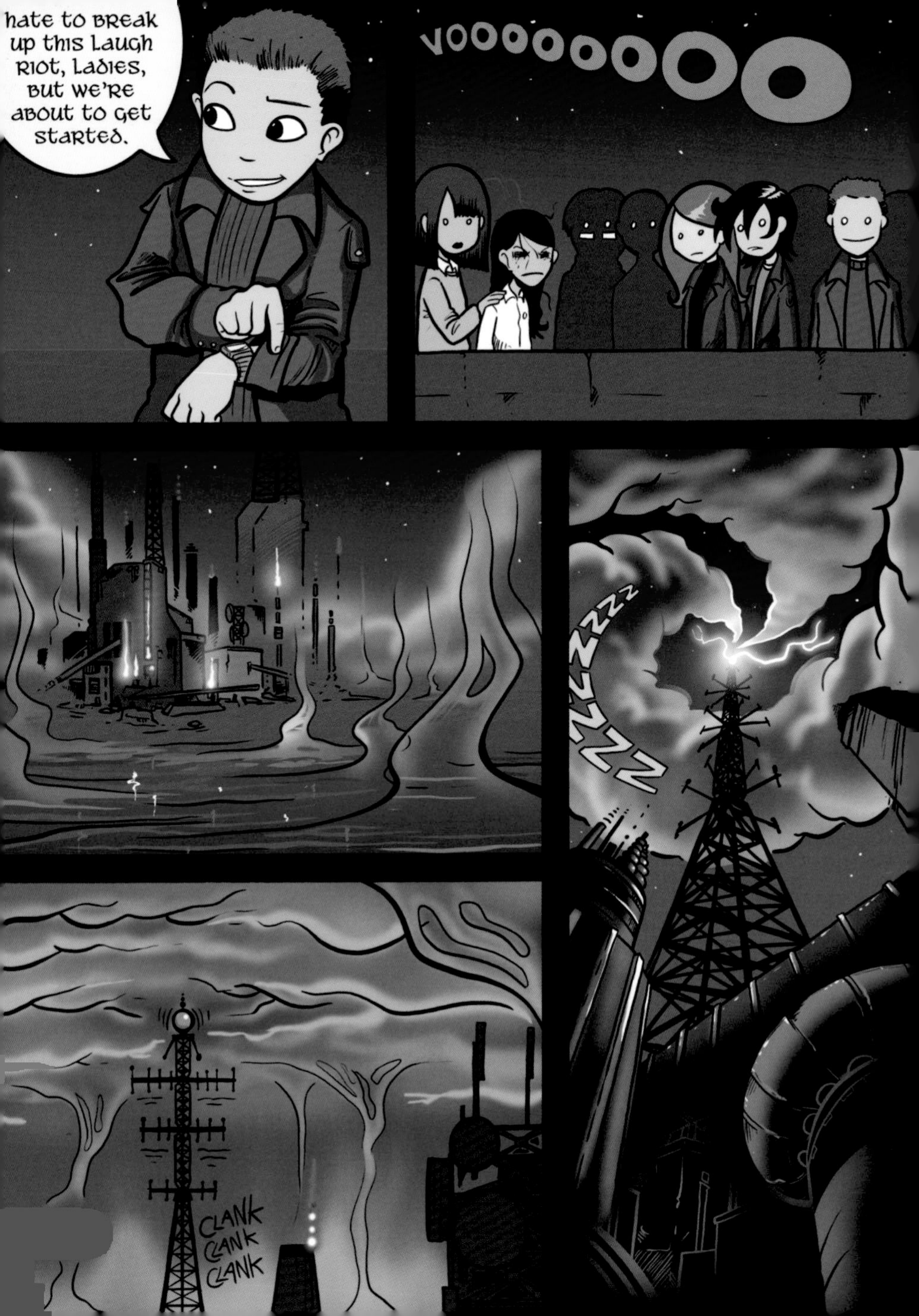
hate to break up this laugh riot, ladies, but we're about to get started.
VOOOOOOOOO
ZZZZZZZZZZ
CLANK CLANK CLANK

CRACK
ZAP

WOW!

CRACK
hey look, the water in the lake is going down.

I bet that's how the clouds are forming.

ZAP

it shot some kind of beam into the horizon!
there must be a receiving station somewhere farther into the court!

huf
huf

Oh, by the way, guys.
CLICK

there's something else I probably should have mentioned...
ZOT

ahhh!
aieee!
eeek!
ahhh!
BOOSH

ahahaha!
you jerk ass.

say, your friend over there doesn't look too well.

wuh...

it...
it ain't working!

it ain't working!

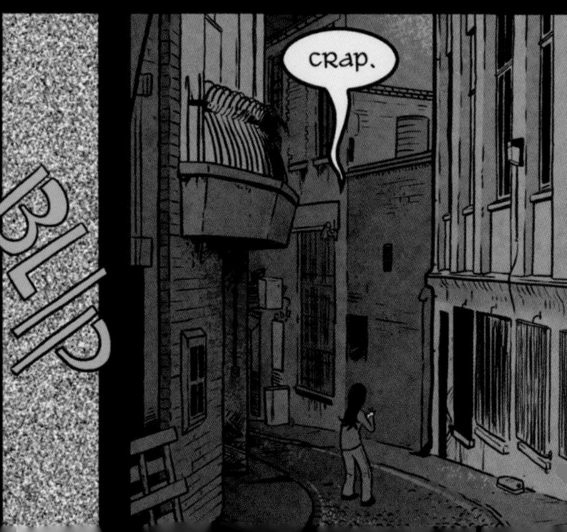
BLIP
crap.

zimmy?! what happened?
oh, you's here too? damn, this was a big one.
that power plant sure messed things up good.
thems other guys is prob'ly stuck here too.
SMAK SMAK

where are they?
I dunno. around. we just gotta find 'em.

okay, but first we find kat.

pfft, no way. first thing we do is look fer gamma.
and some of yer other friends might be closer than donlan so...
first we find kat.

fine!

But yer gonna have ta take Gamma's place.
doing what?

Gettin' ridda these guys.

who are all these people?

they ain't people, they're **nobodies**.

an-an' I ain't goin' nowhere 'less you clear a path.

Jus'... jus' get ridda them, like Gamma does.

um...

GOP

Good. Let's get goin'
Do you see these people around all the time?

Yeah, it can be hard to tell who's real and who ain't.
But these... things don't have faces.

So? Sometimes real people don't neither.

GOP
GOP
how interesting.

GOP
Glad yer havin' fun.

you have a strange gift, zimmy. have you thought about controlling it?

a gift?

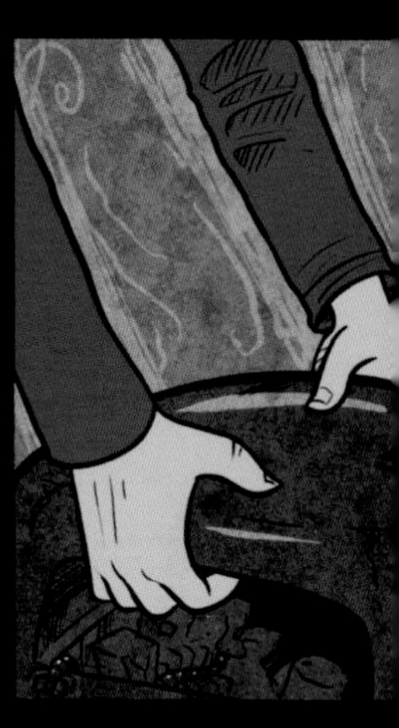

SCRASH
controllin' it?!

you think I want to be like this?!

you think I can't turn all this off cos I's **lazy**?!

you think I want to be...
L~like this...

ah... huh~huh huuuh
Guh~Gamma...
She's the only reason I'm still alive...

you care about her a lot, don't you?

Care about 'er?
I **love** her!

I'd kill everyone in the world and then **myself** if she wanted it!
KICK

that's pretty sweet, except for the part where you kill everyone.

kat!

hey.
I heard you guys miles away.

despite my silky smooth entrance, I'm like five minutes from flippin' out if we don't get out of here, annie.

then we leave. where do we find gamma?
snff.
ain't far.

I thought the rain would have helped you, like it did before.

huh. I guess it didn't cos the rain was fake.
like a shower. them's don't help neither.

you seem okay right now. considering Gamma isn't around.

that's cos she's standin' right next to me.
In real life, I mean.
we's still on that roof.

CKRICK
CRACK

I ain't never gonna be able to leave this damn place.
I'll die here one day.

CRACK
this used to be a toy shop.
Long time ago.
then they came an' gutted it.
now it's miniskirts an' pushup bras, heh.
It took 'em a while to clear out the stock, see.
an' Gamma an' me used to sneak in at night.
she always remembers it.
so when we get split up, we meet back here.

she says she's pretty sure nunna yer other friends ended up here.
just you, carver.

j~just me?

no, kat! don~
GOP
BIP

haha, oh man!
I'm soaked!

annie?
haha!

you look kinda pale...
are you okay?

kat...
???

It's only as real as you let it be.

what the
hell?!

...

oh. you was there
too, huh?

well, sucks
to be you,
mate.

huh?
what was
that about?

Jeez, what a freak.
She's in Chester, right? I heard they are all a bunch of weirdos.
Oh man, look at the time. We better hit the road.
Uh... I~uh, I mean, it was~ I had a... a, you know...
M~me too!
See ya, Jack.
Yeah... yeah.
Say, where are Willie and Janet?
We are here!
We were not doing anything!

pretty weird night.

yes, more questions as to what this place really is.
? ?
heh.

and I think I might know someone who would be willing to give some answers.

Gunnerkrigg Court

Time For Music

hey, john. mind if I come in?
course not, margo.

Gunnerkrigg Court

Chapter 20:

Coyote Stories

oh stop your blithering, child. a little dirt never hurt anyone.
Corneille
Le Cid
I'm just saying you're beginning to get a little grubby.
understatement!
you know my mother made that wolf toy for me. you should take better care of it.
surma made this body?!
hmmm, perhaps I could freshen up a little...

Okay, how do I look?
super hot! you'll knock 'em dead!
Why are you dressed formally!?
Because today I am going to visit coyote in Gillitie forest.
What?!
so soon?!
I... wuh.. you...
Is there a problem?
...
no...
then I'll see you both when I get back.
Remember to do whatever kat tells you.
Guess who's going in the washing machiiine!

are you sure?
yes. I don't think that will be necessary.
okay, well.
at least change your tie for a clip-on.
no need to walk into the forest with a noose about your neck.
ahem.
try not to undress the female students, James.

oh...
oh god...
I~uh, also need... get...
ready...
SLAM
CRIK
is the forest really so dangerous?
CLONK
no, but he worries about you. he wishes he could protect you himself.
excuse
do you know what you will talk to coyote about?
not... not really. I just wanted to pay him a visit.
very well. though it would be a good opportunity to ask him any questions you might have about the court.
In case you were wondering, that is.
ah... right.

ugh, haven't worn this getup in ages.
has anja shown you how to use your blinker stone yet?
no, she sent the signal up for me.
well, no need to keep them waiting.

I don't think so.
do you really need all those swords?
formal attire. you know how it is.
for a dragon slayer?
haha! well, that's just an official title. dragons don't really need slaying so much these days.

here.

take this.

at the first sign of trouble, snap this beacon.
wherever you are, I'll be able to find you and be there within five seconds.

I don't think there will be trouble.

humour me.

thank you.

EVENING, GENERAL.
HELLO, MR. YSENGRIN.
EGLAMORE STAYS HERE. HE IS NOT WELCOME.

carver?
that's fine. I doubt I will be very long.
hurff. taking orders from a little girl, SIR eglamore?

you. you will take me to coyote now.

...

Scratch
Scratch

see the mighty trees, the strong bones of my body!
the rustling of the leaves is my laughter!
the swaying grass is the hair on my back!
the rocks and stones, powerful teeth of mine!
my blood, the water coursing through the land!
my ever watching eyes, the sun...
and the moon!

thank you, coyote, that was very nice.

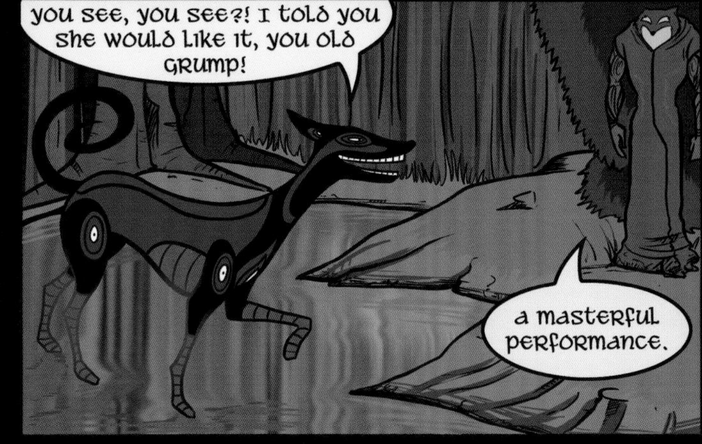
you see, you see?! I told you she would like it, you old grump!
a masterful performance.

yes, I think so too.
yes.

FIRE head GIRL!
welcome to my forest!
no doubt your mother has told you about our time together!

I'm sorry.
she told me stories **about** you, but I did not know you were friends.

ah, tell me which of these stories you like!

hahahaha!
she told me how you placed the stars in the sky.
look how messy they are! It is my fault!
I admit it!
I came across the great spirit placing the stars in the sky one by one...
how boring!
so I told him I would help and began to make beautiful pictures of all the great beasts!
but I am too wise and clever to be entertained by such a menial task for long!
I threw the rest of the stars in the sky and ran about my business!
but look! I forgot to make a picture of myself!
I howl at them all the time in my sadness!
ar! ar ar! arroooo!
ar! ay! ee! ayay! ay! ayyy! ip!

she also said you vere fond of juggling your eyeballs.
ahahaha! yes!
the pretty girls all love when I juggle!
the lovely surma would roll and laugh!
twigs in her hair!
dirt on her bare feet!
It is sad she is gone.
PLOP
PLOP
we are all sad.

all the people of the forest, and there are many.
oh! um, thank you.
but now, **you** are here, and we hope friendship can be born anew!
I hope so too.

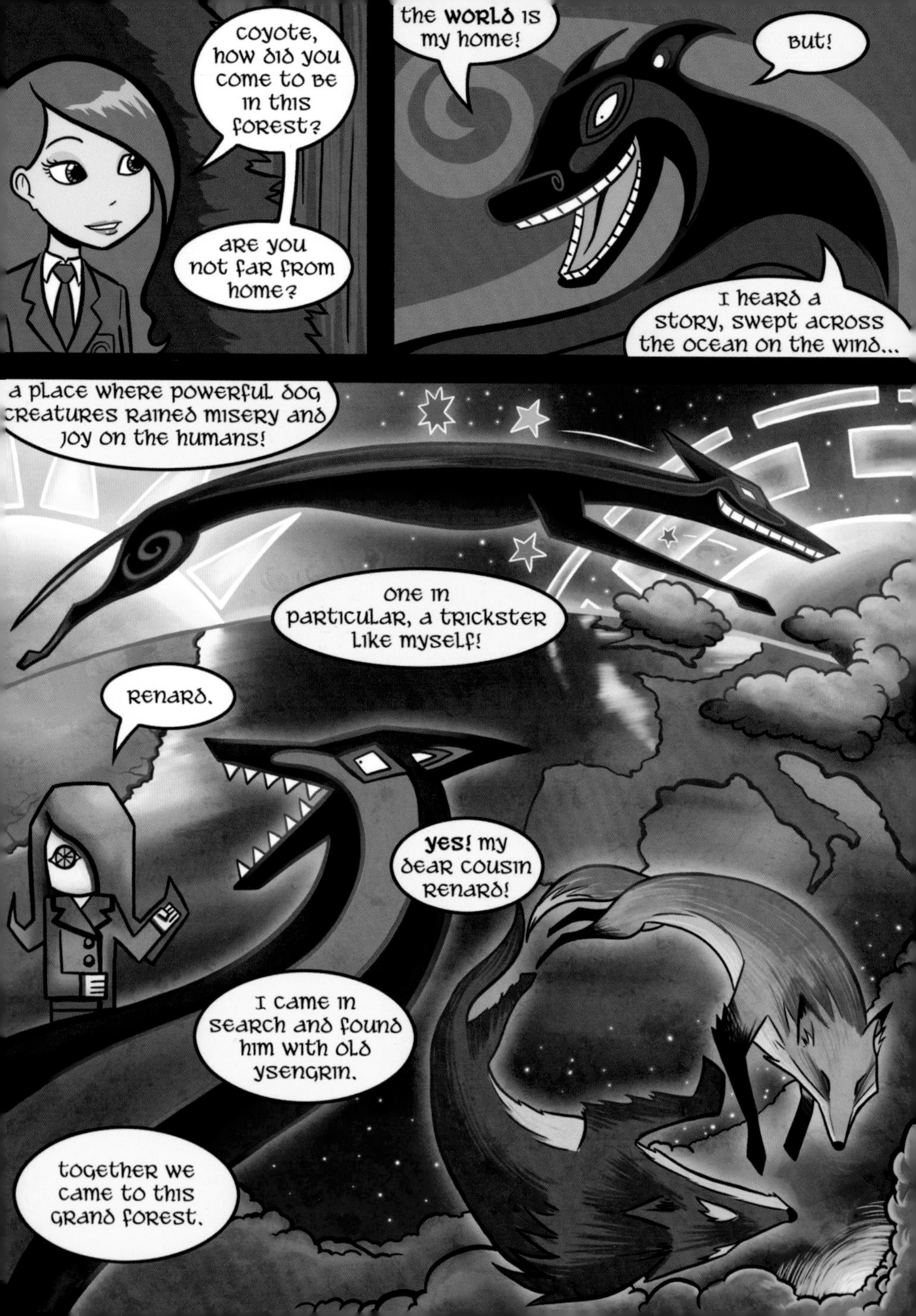
coyote, how did you come to be in this forest?
are you not far from home?
the WORLD is my home!
But!
I heard a story, swept across the ocean on the wind...
a place where powerful dog creatures rained misery and joy on the humans!
one in particular, a trickster like myself!
Renard.
yes! my dear cousin Renard!
I came in search and found him with old ysengrin.
together we came to this grand forest.

this was to be a place of great power, a place of union!
But all we found was a terrible squabble!
the humans sought to tame the powerful creatures!
with my mighty paw I scored the earth and so the court and the forest were divided!
you made the annan waters and the ravine?
yes! I am very powerful, of course.
of course.

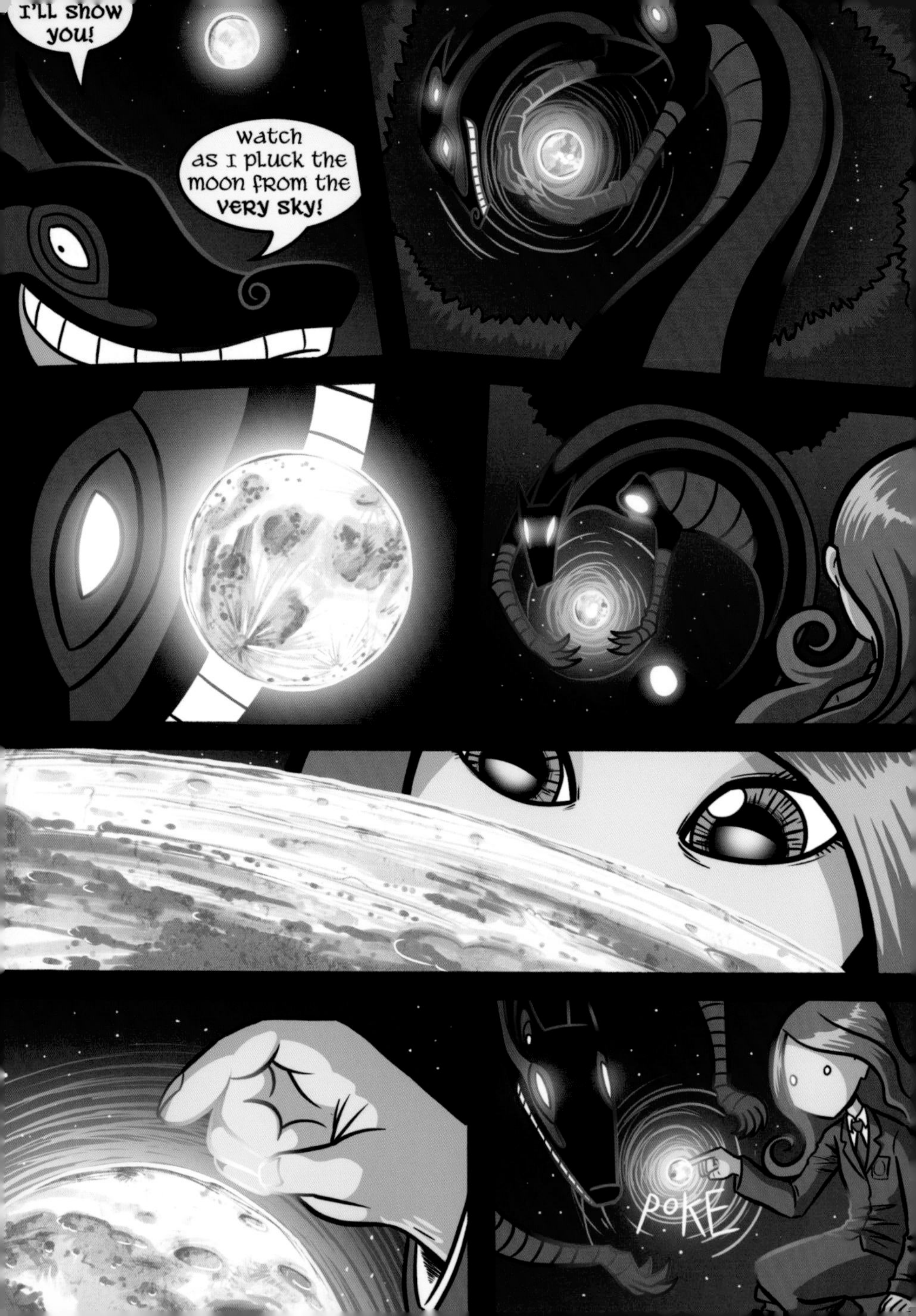
I'LL SHOW YOU!
watch as I pluck the moon from the VERY SKY!
POKE

CHOMP!

w-was that real?

haha! you experienced it, didn't you? what do you think?

you divided the court and the forest...
but now there is a bridge across the annan waters.

the court had done something to the flowing river, and nothing could cross.
eventually a bridge was made, on their terms.

you see, humans sometimes grow weary of their life.
they yearn for something different.
a new life.
with new bodies.
and, when they shun their humanity, we welcome them here.

Is this the test I've heard about?

there is a test, yes.
some creatures of the forest wish to be human, also.

traitors.

haha, it was ysengrin's idea to no longer allow humans into the forest.
not without giving up their bodies first.

have humans lived here before, then?
oh yes! when I divided the forest and court there were some humans and creatures living on both sides.

many of the current inhabitants are descended from those humans.

Why were you looking for Renard in the first place? Why bring him here?
I sought to make him in to a powerful being such as myself!
I wanted to give him my powers, but he would refuse!
He didn't want anything that would widen the gap between himself and the friends he had made amongst the humans.
But why is Reynardine being **held** at the court?
Why, he killed that young man, of course!

I... I assume Reynardine has killed many people.

Oh no! no, no, **nooo!**
Renard **loooves** humans!
not like Ysengrin, who would destroy the lot of them, given the chance.

he tried to kill **me,** once. he tried to take my body.

well now **that** doesn't sound right!
not **you,** of all people!

Why, I wouldn't be surprised if he cared deeply for you!

You see, Renard fell desperately in love with Surma!

after all these years of refusing my powers, he comes to me one day and asks for the ability to take bodies!
overjoyed, I give him the power, but he soon runs away!
he steals the body of a handsome young man and disappears into the court, looking to woo the fiery surma.
how we cried!
we heard he was captured. **tricked!**
one of my own, tricked!
and I did not see him again 'til last summer.
what a surprise to find him with the daughter of surma!

the power I gave Renard was imperfect.
Why, I could control anything with eyes and leave them unharmed when I'd had my fun!
But for some reason, when Renard had the ability, any body he took that was not his own would die when it was used up.
Ysengrin too. I gave him power over the trees, but look how he shakes like an **old man**!
It is a perfect gift.
Immeasurable in its wonder.
Ysengrin loves me very much!

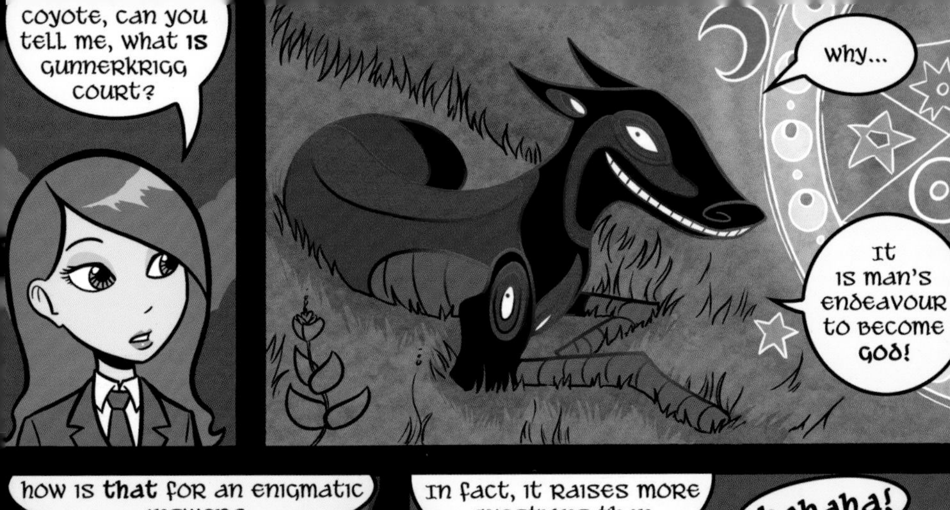
coyote, can you tell me, what **IS** GUNNERKRIGG COURT?
why...
It is man's endeavour to become **GOD!**

how is **that** for an enigmatic answer?
very enigmatic. It barely answers anything at all.

In fact, it raises more questions than before.
hahaha!

aw come on, I can't tell you **everything** right away!
that would make for a boring story, don't you think?

hmm,
that is all
for tonight,
I think!
But...
yes!
goodbye,
fire head!

please come and visit
us whenever you
like!

thank you for your
hospitality,
coyote.

maybe one day
I will tell you
my great
secret!
hahahaha!

hurff...

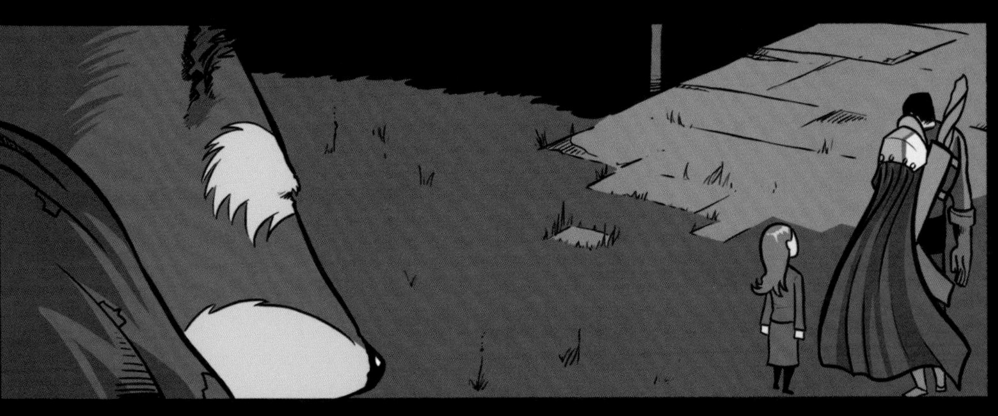

haha, you should see the poor guy. he came out all curly!

he took a hair brush and was all
"leave me beeee!"

hmmm.

welp, I dunno what you were looking for, but there hasn't been any irregular lunar activity recorded over the past few hours.

everything's the same as it always is.
TAP TAP

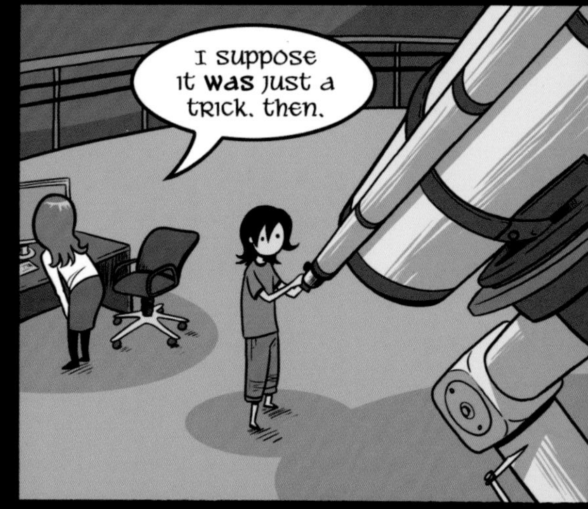
I suppose it **was** just a trick, then.

huh?
Whaa??
that... that can't be right!
ah.
I may have some explaining to do.

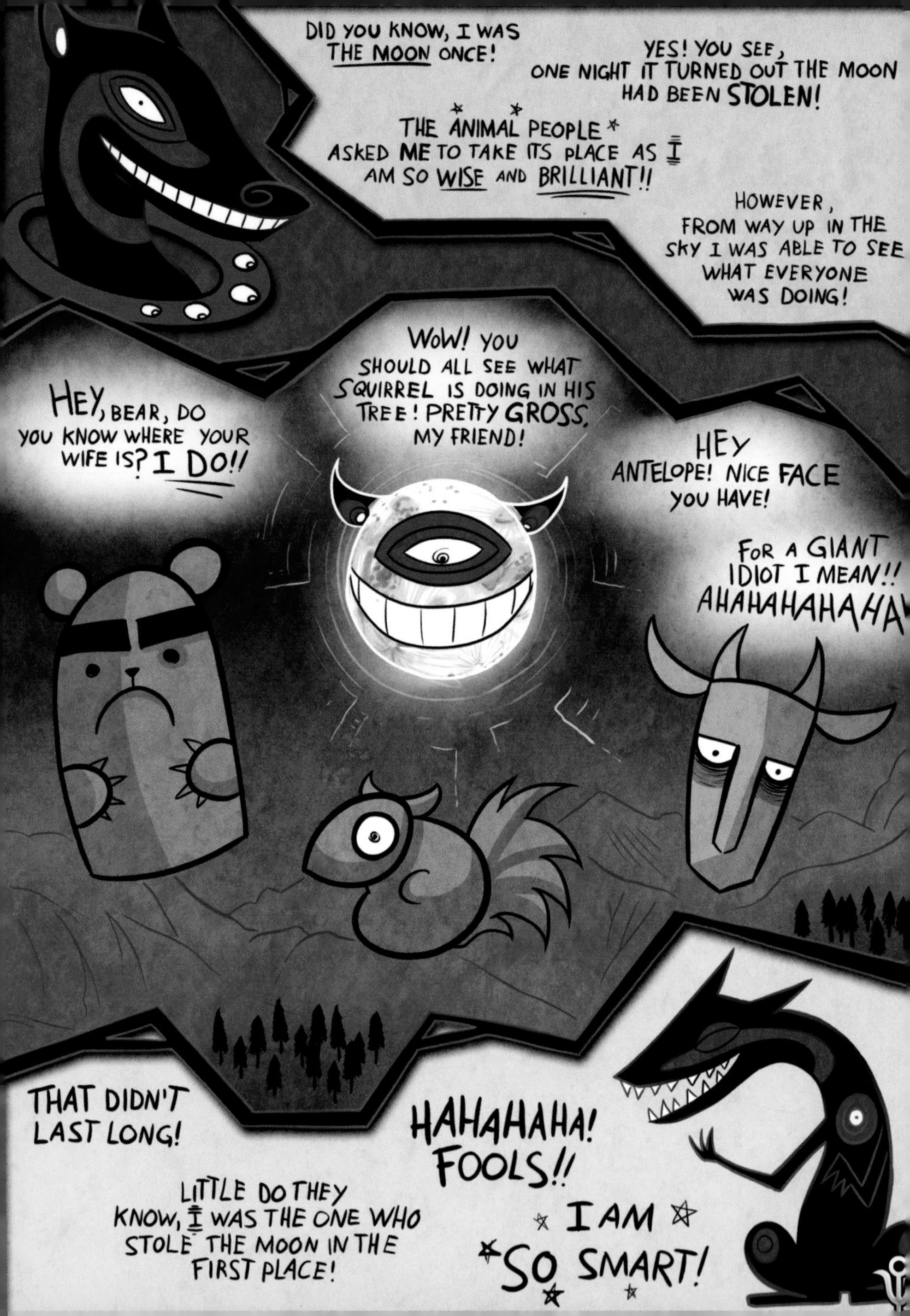

DID YOU KNOW, I WAS THE MOON ONCE!
YES! YOU SEE, ONE NIGHT IT TURNED OUT THE MOON HAD BEEN STOLEN!
THE ANIMAL PEOPLE ASKED ME TO TAKE ITS PLACE AS I AM SO WISE AND BRILLIANT!!
HOWEVER, FROM WAY UP IN THE SKY I WAS ABLE TO SEE WHAT EVERYONE WAS DOING!
HEY, BEAR, DO YOU KNOW WHERE YOUR WIFE IS? I DO!!
WOW! YOU SHOULD ALL SEE WHAT SQUIRREL IS DOING IN HIS TREE! PRETTY GROSS, MY FRIEND!
HEY ANTELOPE! NICE FACE YOU HAVE!
FOR A GIANT IDIOT I MEAN!! AHAHAHAHAHA
THAT DIDN'T LAST LONG!
HAHAHAHA! FOOLS!!
LITTLE DO THEY KNOW, I WAS THE ONE WHO STOLE THE MOON IN THE FIRST PLACE!
I AM SO SMART!

Gunnerkrigg Court

Chapter 21:

Blinking

Oh awesome,
my cnc is here.
set it
down over there,
boys.
ma'm.

hmm. nope, nope.
this isn't very sophisticated.
you are amazing, kat. I can't get my head around any of this.
ah, it's nothing. I just see the tools I got, and the materials, and it just clicks together.

ms. jones said everyone here has a special skill, so I bet this is yours.
here.

Oh... thank you.
...
Jeezum what's up with you two! You've been tip-toeing around each other for ages!
Come on now, be friends again!
CLICK!
Be friends!
Click
Click!
Pat
Pat
...
...

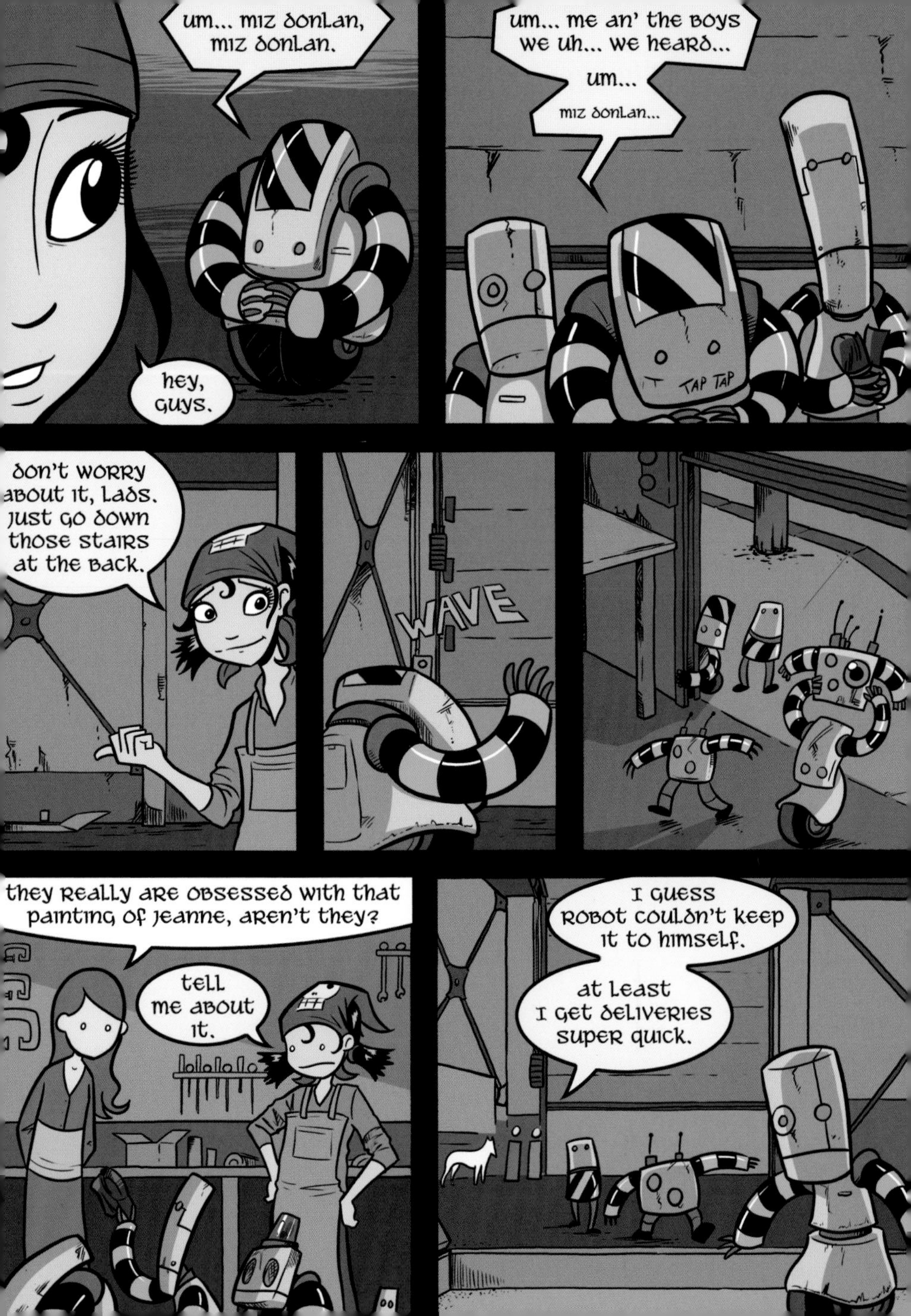
um... miz donlan, miz donlan.
hey, guys.
um... me an' the boys we uh... we heard...
um...
miz donlan...
TAP TAP
don't worry about it, lads. just go down those stairs at the back.
WAVE
they really are obsessed with that painting of jeanne, aren't they?
tell me about it.
I guess robot couldn't keep it to himself.
at least I get deliveries super quick.

knock knock!
mum!
hello, girls.
Reynardine.
anja.
helloooo!
the robots still milling around to see the painting?
yeah, they're always stopping by.

robox is pretty awesome though.
so! I think it's time to learn a little more about your blinker stone, annie. what do you say?

yes, thank you.

okay, first thing's first. did you know that you can never lose a blinker stone?
watch.

I left my stone in my jewelry box at home...

and yet...
BLINK

mommm! that's such a corny trick! you just palmed it.

okay then, here.

hold on to it tightly.

tada!
!
BLINK

now you try, annie. let me take your stone for a moment.

Okay, close your eyes.
Now picture the stone in your mind.
I see it...
Very clearly.
Y~yes... I can see it.
Now try to picture what is around the stone.
You know it's in my hand, so it should be easy.
Carefully try and imagine yourself touching it.
BLINK
It's gotta be some kind of matter transferance!

VERY GOOD!
Okay, another TEST!
haha, okay, I hid your stone outside!
now, even if you have no idea where your blinker is, you will be able to find it.
just close your eyes...
and see the stone.

I can see...
a surface, some dirt... moss.
the wind...
the roof. the stone is on the roof.
very good.
before you pick it up, how far can you see?
I can see into the horizon.
there are so many colours coming from the direction of the forest...
ooh! you're a natural! most people can only focus on a very small area.
Fumble

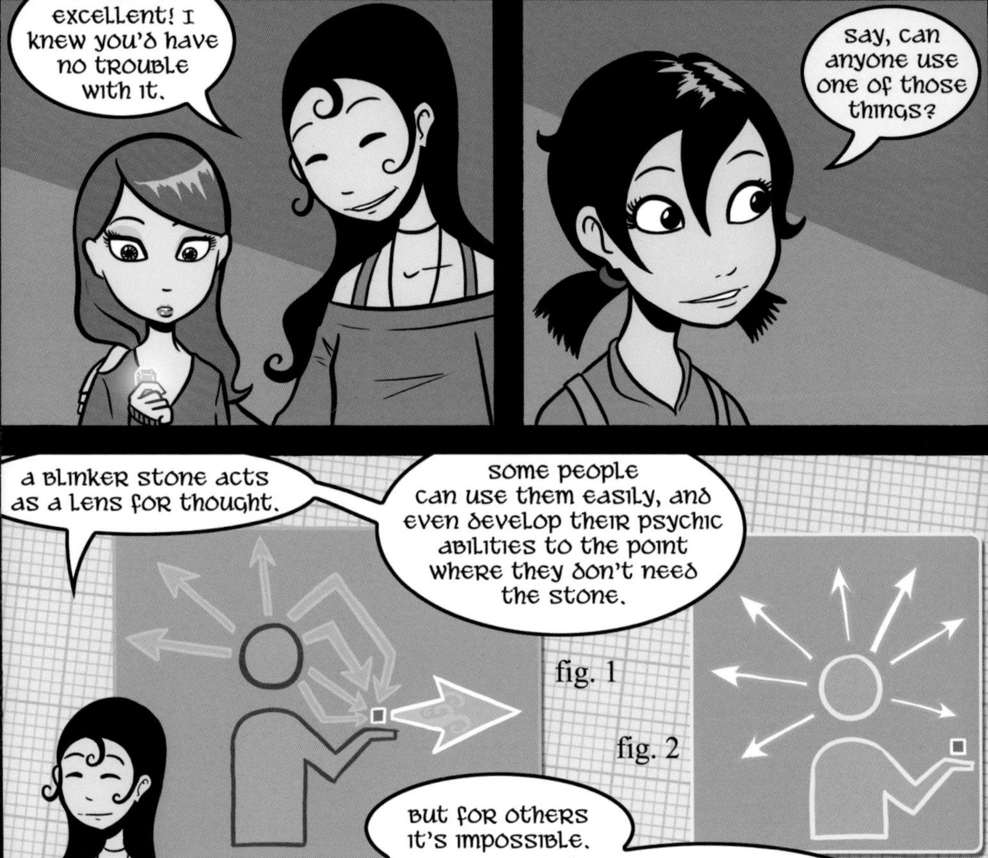
excellent! I knew you'd have no trouble with it.
say, can anyone use one of those things?
a blinker stone acts as a lens for thought.
some people can use them easily, and even develop their psychic abilities to the point where they don't need the stone.
fig. 1
fig. 2
but for others it's impossible.

jones can't use them, which is why she couldn't teach you herself, annie.

your father can't use them either, katja.

anja, are you a magician of some sort?

huh?
oh!

well, you were the best person to show me how to use the blinker stone.
and I've seen you do unexplainable things in the past...
such as when you were able to restrain Reynardine.

and the pendant around your neck. I've seen that symbol before.

oh... hmm...

...

why don't we go talk in the office?
?

tell me, do you girls believe in magic?

heh, of course n
yes.

what? come on, magic is just something that hasn't been explained yet.

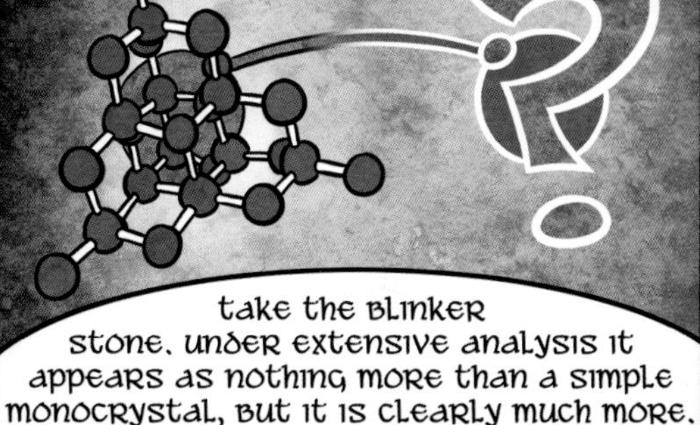
but what would you call something that can't be explained by scientific methods?
take the blinker stone. under extensive analysis it appears as nothing more than a simple monocrystal, but it is clearly much more.

okay, so there just isn't a process to explain how it works yet.

no **scientific** process, perhaps, but there are other methods of explanation. for a long time people thought **alchemy** was a valid methodology.
others may call these methods "**magic**".
the court, on the other hand prefers to define them as "**etheric sciences**".

however, what you saw when I restrained Reynardine...
or rather, this.
ZOOP!

is a program designed to stop him using his body snatching powers.

a program?

specifically, this symbol is the program.
your father and I designed it together, Katja.

huh? how can a glowing... floaty... symbol be a program? what runs it?

this pendant is actually a soft link to a computer I built. It houses the program developed to keep Renard in check.

I never really see you using computers...
Well, my computer is a very specialised piece of equipment, tucked away in a safe location. I can access it remotely, using my pendant, and information is sent to me directly.
Donald is a sub-user on the system.
That's how he was able to produce a shield when Ysengrin became riled last summer, Annie.
But what did you use to jargon jargon babble babble strange words?
Haha, it took a while to perfect, but chatter chatter jargon computers technical wizardry babble jargon.

anja forgot to mention that spying with a blinker stone is not recommended.

Blink
um... people have been using symbols to invoke or ward off spirits for a long time.

that's right. the principle is the same here.
James has a tattoo of the symbol, which protected him from Renard in the past.

Mr. Eglamore has a tattoo?!
yes. and your dad.
I tattooed them both myself.

huhh??
what?
ah yes, good times. good times!

Reynardine's power was bestowed by coyote himself...
yet you found a way to manipulate it using technology?
well, yes and no.
my computer is based on work we did finding a way to control Reynardine.
however, just like the blinker stone, there is a lot about the etheric process we just can't understand.
basically, we cheated
the computer is a hybrid of court technology and just enough etheric technology to allow it to work.
because of this, though, the court sees it as a useless system.
that's not fair... I mean, it works, right?
some say that isn't good enough. not if you can't fully explain **how** it works.

so, annie, I have to ask, who was the boy that gave you your stone?
um... his name is mort.
but how did you know it was a boy?
haha! blinker stones are traditionally given between couples.
donald gave me mine a long time ago.
oh maaann! I knew it!
I see.
anyway, what say I show you a few more tricks?

ahaha! mort is such a sweetheart!
It has been a while since we last saw him.
yay!
oh, hey guys!
what uh... what brings you round my neck o' the woods?
hehe...
I suppose you think this was funny.
huh?

you thought you could stake some sort of claim on me?
without me knowing?
did you?
well you can have it back!
SLAM
annie!
what the hell?? what the hell was that?!
you don't throw a gift back in someone's face like that!
especially if it's from a boy who likes you!
he's not a boy, kat. he's just a ghost.
annie!

Look, uh... It wasn't my idea.
Mort...
Muut appeared the night you fell off the bridge and started telling me it would be a good idea to send you something.
Like, a gift you would find useful.
But... afterlife guides aren't allowed to interfere with the living world.
I know. He kept making out it was **my** idea, even though he had the stone right there.
I mean, I didn't even know what the thing was, but it was **Muut**, what could I say?
I guess it was pretty important you got it.

But why a blinker stone?

Yeah, how would I know?
I'm just a ghost.

BWIP

oh, annie… I think he heard you…
mort?
mort?
mort I…
c'mon. I think you should make yourself scarce.
Dulce et Decorum

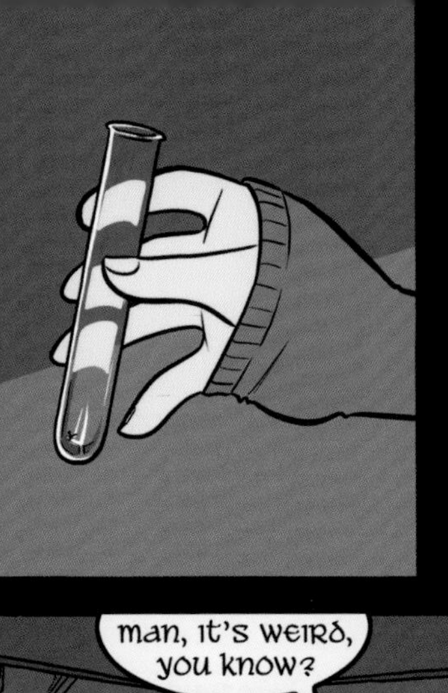

TAP
TAP

man, it's weird, you know?

I mean, it's just an ant...
But now that I know there is some creepy insect guy that appears when it dies makes this kinda hard to~

oh.
squish

uh... just make sure I can't see this click~clack guy again.

hello, ketrak.

sorry to bother you. could you get muut for me, please?
you should not have wasted a life in such a way.
If you have a better way to contact you, I'm all ears.

also, you should make yourself visible to my friend, kat. no need to be rude.

why did you tell mort to give this to me? since when do **you** bend the rules?
we needed your help.
the girl you saw that night...
she has been there a very long time.
alone.
waiting.
we are powerless to help her.
we do not even know who she is.
her name is jeanne.
then you have already begun to help.
we knew you would.
It was only a matter of time.

If you are so clever, why didn't you just **ask** me to help?
Would you have agreed, had the request come from **us**?
Why a blinker stone?
Think of it as a first step.
A means to extend your reach beyond the material world...
Into the world in which Jeanne resides.
Lost, stranded in the aether, she needs a hand like yours to be an anchor.
Is that all?
Wait...

what's the deal with you guys?

why are you so mad at them, annie? is it 'cos... one of them had to take your mom?

tell her.
?

the night surma passed on...
none of us came for her.

but...
then...
oh no...

I had to do it myself.

...
Bap

thank you, kat.
no problem.

now I ask a tiny favour of you.

you know we are not allowed to interfere in the living realm.

no need to worry about that.

ELSEWHERE.
WE ARE HERE TO DESTROY YOUUU!
ahhhhhhh!
ahhhhhhh!
ahhhhhhh!

It is a jest.
In reality we are here to deliver this.
aaaaahhhhhhhh
what.
ooh, a card!
It has a heart on it.
Mort
Dearest, Mort
I am very sorry.
I am a terrible fool.
Please forgive me.
with love,
Antimony
(also: BOO)
carver sent you?!
yes.
hahaha!
what the hell, annie?
HA HA HA HA HA
Silenti
HA HA HA HA!

Gunnerkrigg Court
Reynardine The Sheep

Gunnerkrigg Court

Chapter 22:

Ties

CHACK

aright, be off with you.
stick your names down on the form.

any other groups want their picture takin'?

We do!
PHOTOS

I bet it looks stupid!
I always look so serious in photos!

I bet I had on me serious face!

Oh sush!
You look beautiful!
And is nice to have picture of friends!

You mean picture of **Donny!**

But he is soooo handsome!

You mean a picture of Anja! Hahaha!
Aww, come on, man.

haha! don't worry about it, man.

I wish jones could have been in the photo, though.
eh, you know surma can't stand her.

yeah...

hey, tony, aren't you coming for lunch?

I have matters to attend to.

oh... okay. we'll see you later, then.
Nod

"I have matters to attend to."
jeez, who talks like that?

won't you stay a little longer, Brinnie?

SORRY!
you know how the old man get angry when I skip lesson.

Is such stupid thing, we can not even have lunch together anymore.
But what can you do?!

I will see you later!

you tell me how photo-picture comes out!
ZAM

who let the freakshow in here?

I'll never get used to that!
Heh! Brinnie is such a show off!

shoulda left them in chester, with the other weirdos.
Ha ha, yeah

say that to me face, hyland, I dare ya!

alright, you an' your friends are **freaks**, how's that, you cu~

WHUD

Jimmy!
hyland, get out of my sight.
eglamore, my office. now.

Bah! you shoulda zapped him, anja!
CREAK
woulda teached him!

?
um... excuse please, donald!

dang it, jimmy.
what's the matter, love?
surma, you know people they don't like when we use our magics!

things are different in queslett. they get angry.
so what? stuff 'em!
It's not like we're the only ones with a "predetermination towards etheric sciences."
the court made a mistake when they put us in chester. they said so!
everything's fine now.
but that was so long ago. and still people do not forget! people fear what is strange to them.
this is about donny, isn't it?
he's our friend, anny. he doesn't care about that.

fine, fine.
But one day you'll realise you don't hafta hide who you are just to fit in.
no matter what anybody says.
Look's like it's just us three for lunch then!

TWIST

LOOK, SIR,
HYLAND STARTED IT! HE'S A JACKASS!
I'M NOT BLIND, OR STUPID.
I KNOW HOW PEOPLE ARE AROUND HERE.

BUT THAT DOESN'T EXCUSE WHAT YOU DID.
HAD ANY OTHER TEACHER BESIDES ME STOPPED YOU, YOU MIGHT BE FACING EXPULSION.

YOU REALISE THAT, RIGHT?

YES SIR...
BUT STILL.

STANDING UP FOR A FRIEND. A NOBLE ACT CANNOT BE DISMISSED.
!

you fly off the handle too quickly, James.
you need to keep your temper in check.
yes, sir.
you have a future here, and I don't want to see you ruin your chances.
sir?

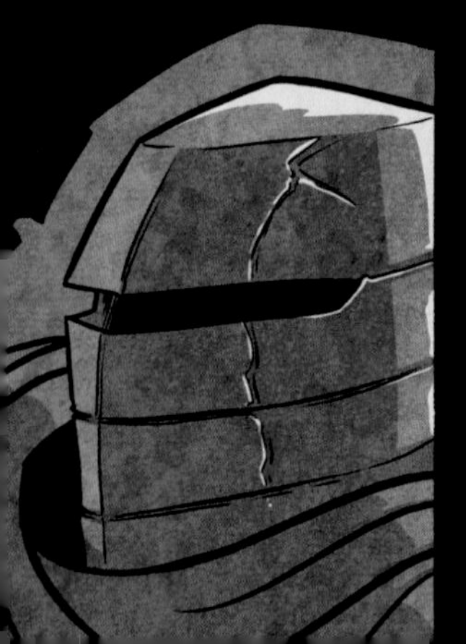

have you ever heard of the Rogat Orjak?

WOOP
WOOP
CLANK
CLANKY
halt! this exit is now closed!
WOOP
WOOP
please use this other exit and go about your business.
there is currently a situation.

WOOP
WOO
the situation does not involve a large monster or two.
man, shut uuuup!

Don't see those robots very often
Model B, yes?

CRASH
SMASH

c'mon,
we **have** to get
a better look
at this!
ROOF
hold it
right there,
you crazy
kids!

shoo! get back!
away! go on!

Pip Pip

BEWwww

quick! make 'em face the other way! the disruptor only lasts a few seconds.

there...
Bing!

yes! we shall leave now! thank you! good job!

y~yes, you do... that.
wow, ace job, boss!
So cool!

...just something I put together. Harmless.

there it is!

It's like some kinda dog!
a dog made of wood...

NNNNNNNN

I think it's just trying to get through!

Is... is not a real creature. Is more like... puppet... being called back to forest.

huh? how can you tell?

uh... umm...

maybe it's like a drone or something.

Look out!
SPANG

INCREDIBLE!
OH! WELL...
UH, CAN YOU GUYS SAVE IT FOR LATER?
CHONK

ZMMMMMMM
CHFF
hi,
guys.

Don't forget Double Cross Country tomorrow, James.
Oh... Right.

JIMMY?! WHAT'S GOING ON?
YOU GUYS AREN'T GOING TO BELIEVE THIS...
BUT THAT GUY IS OUR GAMES TEACHER.

VISIT the
STARS

City Face #1

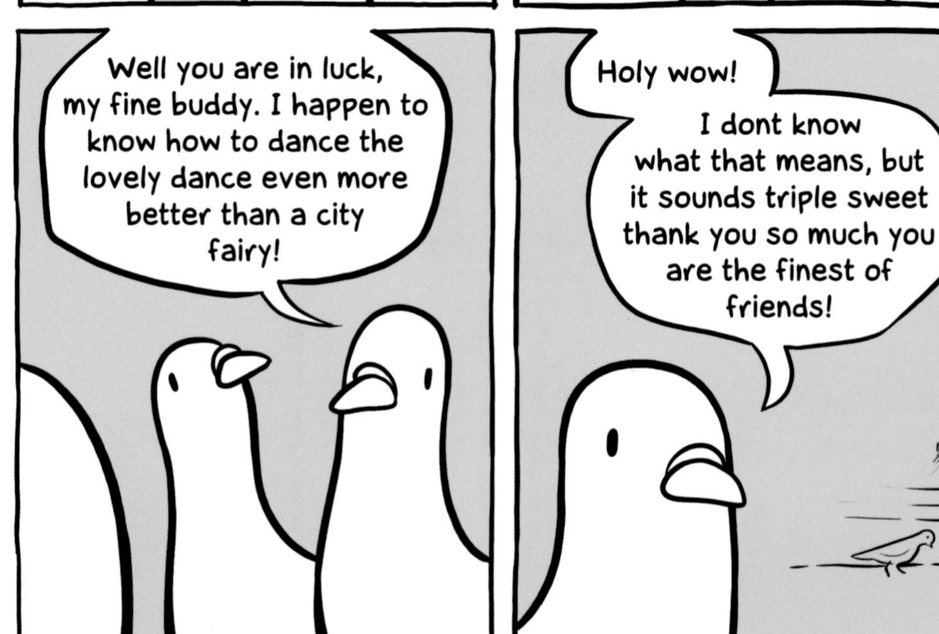

www.gunnerkrigg.com

City Face #2

www.gunnerkrigg.com

City Face #3

Polo! Why are you such a good dancer?

Just as the dirt and grime encrusts the city, and the stone of life grinds us all to dust, so will I always rule the fairy dancing circle!

And why is Lightfoot so bad at dancing?
Lightfoot
That's because she is a meanie-bo-beanie with a dumb stupid face and her face needs to shut up forever!

City Face #4

Mustard Seed!
I gotta go give the gift of dance to an individual in need!

Oh!
Where will you be back?
Right here!

See you in an inch!
ZWINK

Meanwhile
siiiiiiiiiigh

City Face #5

www.gunnerkrigg.com

City Face #6

!

CLIP

Ehehe!
It wer a joke, mate!

What? What was a joke? Is the excellent joke in your mouth too? I didn't get a super good look I'm sorry, can I look again?
I was just a little nervous before on account of your many, many fine sharp fangs.

City face #7

TADAA! I am Polo and I am here to help you learn the loveliest of dances!

You must be a city fairy! But why do you want to help a pigeon as awesome as me? Which is to say, not as awesome as other pigeons??

Feather Face! If you do not charm that girl pigeon with the power of dance, the world... could be DESTROYED!

Oh nooo! Not the world!
That would be just super awful for EVERYBODY!

www.gunnerkrigg.com

City Face #8

More neck feathers!
More!
And bob your head more!
Now spin!
Ahhhhhh!

But also wait! Why would the world be destroyed just because my dancing is not the finest??
It's because of humans!

Humans LOVE pigeons, and if you don't make more baby pigeons they will get so angry and destroy EVERYTHING!

Oh my goshhh!

And I always thought humans did not like pigeons! On account of them always killing us and poisoning us and also laughing and stomping on us until we are dead when they are super drunk sometimes!

City Face #9

Oh my gosh!
Oh my gosh!
Is she looking?

Go on! Keep it up!
You're doing great!

Is she looking??
Oh my gosh I think she is!

Hello. Your dancing is super good and also you have the shinest of neck feathers.
YESSSS!